ANGUS PETER CAMPBELL is fro
Garrynamonie Primary School a.
his English teacher was Iain Crichton Smith. After graduating in Politics and History from the University of Edinburgh he has worked as a kitchen porter, tree planter, builders' labourer, lobster fisherman, journalist and writer.

By the same author:

The Greatest Gift, Fountain Publishing, 1992
Cairteal gu Meadhan-Latha, Acair Publishing, 1992
One Road, Fountain Publishing, 1994
Gealach an Abachaidh, Acair Publishing, 1998
Motair-baidhsagal agus Sgàthan, Acair Publishing, 2000
Lagan A' Bhàigh, Acair Publishing, 2002
An Siopsaidh agus an t-Aingeal, Acair Publishing, 2002
An Oidhche Mus Do Sheòl Sinn, Clàr Publishing, 2003
Là a' Dèanamh Sgèil Do Là, Clàr Publishing, 2004
Invisible Islands, Otago Publishing, 2006
An Taigh-Samhraidh, Clàr Publishing, 2007
Meas air Chrannaibh/ Fruit on Branches, Acair Publishing, 2007
Tilleadh Dhachaigh, Clàr Publishing, 2009
Suas gu Deas, Islands Book Trust, 2009
Archie and the North Wind, Luath Press, 2010
Aibisidh, Polygon, 2011
An t-Eilean: Taking a Line for a Walk, Islands Book Trust, 2012
Fuaran Ceann an t-Saoghail, Clàr Publishing, 2012
The Girl on the Ferryboat, Luath Press, 2013
An Nighean air an Aiseag, Luath Press, 2013
Memory and Straw, Luath Press, 2017
Stèisean, Luath Press, 2018
Constabal Murdo, Luath Press, 2018
Tuathanas nan Creutairean, Luath Press, 2021
Constabal Murdo 2: Murdo ann am Marseille, Luath Press, 2022
Electricity, Luath Press, 2023
Eighth Moon Bridge, Luath Press, 2024

Donald & his Seven Cows

ANGUS PETER CAMPBELL

Luath Press Limited
EDINBURGH
www.luath.co.uk

First published 2025

ISBN: 978-1-80425-208-6

The author's right to be identified as author of this book
under the Copyright, Designs and Patents Act 1988
has been asserted.

Printed and bound by
Clays Ltd., Bungay

Typeset in 12 point Sabon by
Main Point Books, Edinburgh

© Angus Peter Campbell 2025

Contents

Introduction by Angus Martin   7

Donald & his Seven Cows   13

Acknowledgements   207

Introduction

WHEN ANGUS PETER CAMPBELL asked me if I would read and comment on a book he had written, I was slightly apprehensive because it was a work of fiction and I hadn't read a novel or short story since last century.

I agreed, because for many years Angus Peter, whom I have never met, has publicly endorsed my work in both poetry and history, and I'd be a liar if I claimed to be immune to appreciation, since the subjects I choose to write about have never attracted a wide readership. He, as a writer, is perhaps in a similar position, because much of his work has been published in his native Gaelic.

We were both born in 1952, two months apart. His earliest years were spent in South Uist and mine in Kintyre: geographically far apart but once connected by a common language and heritage. A cultural gap between these two communities opened in the nineteenth century. The last Gaelic speakers in my family were John Martin and Sarah Campbell, great-grandparents. When I attended secondary school in Campbeltown in the 1960s, some of the pupils from North Kintyre had native Gaelic-speaking grandparents, but before the end of the century these Gaelic speakers had all died and taken the language with them.

That irreversible force of attrition has now visited

the remotest parts of the *Gàidhealtachd* which had seemed safest. The Uist Angus Peter Campbell grew up in – with Gaelic-speaking crofters on the *machair* lands, planting and weeding and harvesting and tending their stock – now seems to him like a 'dream', and I think that *Donald & His Seven Cows* is essentially about travelling through the landscapes of that dream and back to a beginning which is also – as cycles dictate – an end.

Many of us whose childhoods were happy – or happy enough, I should say – increasingly return in memory, as we age, to the formative places and people of the past. There is now, however, a great difference in the character and degree of that nostalgia, because social and cultural and environmental changes have accelerated at such a rate in the past fifty years that one can almost stand in a long-familiar place, look around and ask, 'Where am I? What has happened?'

Some of us know, and fear, what has happened. There has been a terrible disconnect from the natural world and fewer and fewer people work the land and the sea.

When I grew up in Campbeltown, the fishing industry was thriving and there was a fishing community within the wider community: families which had intermarried for generations, with sons following their father to sea. Most of these boys, unless they were exceptionally academic, didn't consider any other future. But overfishing ruined the herring and white fish industries, and the continuity was broken. The relatively few boats which now work from Kintyre ports are catching shellfish species which, aside from lobster, were dumped over the side as unmarketable a hundred years ago. Instead of a healthy fishing industry, we have miserable fish caged offshore in pollutant 'farms'.

It is the same with agriculture: the community has dwindled; most farmers work the land alone or with a few family members; and old arable fields are rank with rushes or choked with bracken. Alien conifers cover the uplands, with giant wind towers sprouting among them, and the latest gimmick is 'carbon offsetting': the ploughing of good farmland to plant woodland, which, when the time comes that farmers are again needed to do what they always did best, will stand, tree by uneatable tree, as testimony to political ineptitude and capitalist greed.

That's a little of what I know about Kintyre. About the Uist of Angus Peter Campbell's childhood, I know nothing from personal experience, but this book has stories to tell, not only of an inevitably lost childhood but also of a lost community, with its ancient language and culture sacrificed on the altar of 'progress'. The 'ceilidh house' has been replaced with a big television screen on a wall and computers and mobile phones have ushered in a multitude of phantom communities and unmet 'friends' to replace the real community which exists minutes away from the locked door and its blinding 'security light'.

This book is essentially about a day in the life of Donald, who accompanies his seven dairy cows around the croft. In reality, it is unlikely he would have dedicated entire days to the herding of cattle; yet the *buachaille* (herd) of history did just that. He, or she, was usually a child sent out with the cows to keep them from straying on to neighbouring grazings or into fields of growing crops (this at a time when fencing was rudimentary or non-existent).

The reader is witness to a ritualistic round of visitations – transmuted from the Stations of the Cross in Catholic worship – as Donald moves, in his leisurely way, into and out of the past, remembering the dead and meditating on change. Places, naturally, are intrinsic to the journey – as to any journey – but his travels are confined within a small space, and the sights he sees are so familiar to him that he claims to know 'every blade of grass'. An impossibility, to be sure, but one with its roots in truth, for those of the past who worked the land had intimate knowledge of its every feature, and had names for these features: fields, rocks, knolls, ridges, ravines, hollows, springs ... everything. And the names had stories behind them, some forgotten, some obscure, and some remembered.

As I know, from having collected the lore of my native Kintyre from the last tradition-bearers, since the mechanisation of farming and the exodus from the land, most of these minor place-names have died with the families which preserved them. I quote from my book *Kintyre Places and Place-Names*, its source that gloomy memoir, *Night Falls on Ardnamurchan*:

> The poet Alasdair Maclean gave eloquent expression to that loss [of place-names]. As a boy in the township of Sanna, Ardnamurchan, he roamed all over the

neighbourhood, sometimes accompanied by his grandfather, who had a name for 'every least hillock, every creek and gully'. Maclean felt that such knowledge set his grandfather apart, invested him with a 'form of spiritual privilege', so that he 'lived in a different landscape from me, seeing it in a different way and – I came to feel – being seen differently by it'.

I admitted at the start that I hadn't read fiction since last century but didn't give a reason. Here is my attempt at an explanation (not that it should matter to anyone else, except in the frame of this undertaking): perhaps because I've spent most of my life researching and writing social history and reconstructing real lives (as far as 'reality' can be perceived or trusted), I tired of artificial stories and stopped reading them.

Angus Peter Campbell's story is certainly a species of fiction, but the elements of history and folklore and cultural memory kept me interested to the end, and, increasingly, the strange atmosphere of the story put me under its spell.

I suspect that it is not a narrative that will entertain a reader in search of conventional plot development and gratuitous excitement. Rather, it is the diffident, rambling testimony of a man – an *amadan* (fool) in the eyes of his neighbours – who is voluntarily trapped in the past and unwilling to engage with the present or surrender to the future.

Donald & His Seven Cows has perhaps not been written for a mass readership – the title itself is defiant in its mundanity – yet I wish Donald and his little herd well in their journey to the outer world. They carry messages from the past to inform readers in the future that there were (and are) other ways of living and thinking, tried and tested by millennia of down-to-earth experience and supernatural engagement.

Angus Martin
Campbeltown, Kintyre, June 2025

I

I KNOW THIS mile so well. It's a round mile. Like the full moon. Two thousand two hundred and forty yards, by the Gaelic way of counting, beginning from the end of the byre where I walk the cows from every morning round our world. We stop twelve times. Every two hundred and twenty-four steps. These are places where we spend our days.

I know they say a mile is one thousand seven hundred and sixty yards. But not here. They told me that official measure when I went to school but I didn't believe the teacher, because I'd paced it out every day before school with my grandfather and it was two thousand two hundred and forty yards of his steps and four thousand four hundred and eighty yards of mine. I had to take two steps for every one of his, but now that I've walked like him for the past fifty years I can assure you it's two thousand two hundred and forty yards. Even if I have to stretch a bit now to make them. A *ceum* (step) here is two-and-a-half feet.

Maybe I invented the mile. I don't know, for no one else knows it exists. They just see me wandering about as if the cows are leading me, haphazardly, to where grass and more grass is. But no, it's not like that. We lead each other, for we all now know the route, and where the puddles are, and the stones to avoid, and that little stream which freezes over in the winter and the hollow green shade where we all rest in the summer. We go where we all agree to go. The ground is good and solid under my feet. It makes me feel secure. If it didn't, I would just rise and fly off into the air and Maisie and the herd might look at me ascending for a moment and then resume their grazing. Or they might fly off with me and join the great Fingalian cows of the sky that scholars call the Milky Way. The cows are greater than me in so many ways. Stronger. Patient. More productive.

Looking up and looking down are two different things. I tend to look down to see the marks the cows' hooves make in the earth and the way the bell heather is already beginning to bloom though it's hardly beyond the Feast of the Immaculate Heart of Mary, and I have to remind myself to look up to see the flecks of cloud now in a dragon shape on top of the hill and the way the sky is already bright blue far to the north-west. It's a puzzle solved every day. You only see what's there when you're not really looking for it.

It's not that we walk a trail every day, or a marked path. There's liberty. The cows can wander where they want, but over the years they've come to know where they should go, the rocky bits to avoid and where the pastures green lie. By now I'm into the fiftieth generation, so they're born with that knowledge. They move slowly because they have all the time in the world. It takes the full day to travel a mile. We walk sunwise. East, north, south, west. Eternity will be a quiet joyous day like this, herding. Breathing slowly.

It hasn't been easy. For them or me. For me especially, because I've had to mould and shape the mile without leaving any signs, any clues that it's a carefully worked out path. For next thing other people might start using it, and then Morrison the Council Officer will be round with his Jeep putting signs up telling everyone about it. Do Not Enter. Danger This Way. All these signals folk need to have to know what's safe and what's not. A few months ago he asked me to start cleaning up the cows' dung on the round mile because all that dirt would spoil the official walk they're planning to build. It's the future. A walking path without any beasts spoiling their shoes. Once I go, there will be no more cattle. Half the mile with shit bags to keep things tidy. Poop bags, they call them on the notices with those little red boxes for collecting them.

'This place belongs to the herd,' I told him. 'Without them, the earth will die.'

Sometimes I think they're the ones making the earth as they go along, leaving their hoof marks in the grass and mud, chewing up everything that is in front of them and fertilizing it at every second step as they plod forwards. On rare windless days they swing their tails as they graze, to get rid of the flies.

I've had to be careful not to go mad. One year I twisted my knee and went to see Nurse MacLeish and after she examined me, she asked me if I was anxious.

I didn't really know what that meant, so I asked her.

'Do you worry about things?' she said.

'Not much,' I said.

'What kind of things?' she asked.

'My cows,' I said. 'That they won't grow properly.'

She left it at that, but it made me anxious, if that's what it was. For she went on and talked to me about a disease called OCD which meant that people (and I knew fine she meant me) repeated things over and over again because they then feel safe, but the danger is that if the pattern is broken then their whole world falls apart. The knife to the right of the plate, the fork to the left, and the spoon above, or everything is chaos.

That's me all right, but as far as I can make out everyone is like that. Every morning down the road I hear Janet Smith singing and talking to her hens. And every morning in the same order.

'Dearg, tha thu an sin!' ('Red, you're there!')

'Buidhe – ciamar a tha?' ('Yellow – how are you?')

'Gorm, a ghaoil!' ('Blue, my darling!')

'Ugh an-diugh, Uaine?' ('An egg today, Green?')

''ille Dhuibh, robh thu modhail an-raoir?' ('Black lad, did you behave last night?')

Every day like a liturgy, and each one cackles back to her in time. Miss Smith is very pious and goes to all the services, even when they're not on Holy Days of Obligation. Whenever she visits anyone she always knocks three times on their door in the name of the Father, Son, and Holy Ghost, to bless the house and the people in it. I rarely visit anyone, but for a while I also took to knocking three times at the byre door in the morning to bless Maisie and the herd, my beloved treasures. I didn't want to be like Janet though, so I began doing it seven times, adding the names of saints Peter and Paul and Mary and Joseph. Thing is, the herd then took to lying-in and not stirring until they were blessed the seven times, when they'd rise in unison. So I stopped it, knowing they'd be blessed anyway, innocent creatures as they are.

During weekdays Miss Smith walks with one hand over her shoulder as if she's always carrying a sack of potatoes. Her parents and grandparents were potato-merchants, forever transporting tatties on pack-horses from the fields out to the steamship for sale on the mainland. Every day is like a mystery story. How is it that Janet always manages to say the same things, in exactly the same tone of voice, while the hens all cackle back in different ways? I think it depends on the weather. They sound mournful when their feathers are all soaking wet.

And the schoolteacher. I see him driving past every morning, his right hand nonchalantly holding the wheel and his left a cigarette. When the weather is fine, he has the car window open, and I can hear music. It's always the same too: operatic singing, I think they call it. He's also an artist. Converted his old father's byre into a studio and works there after school and sells his paintings on Saturdays. They're all about the sea, painted in a bright blue colour I've never seen in any water. There are no people or cows or sheep or dogs in his pictures. I suppose everyone wants a life free of bother. We know so little about anyone. They hide whole worlds.

Mind you, it's good we're not all the same. Just like Maisie and the herd. They all have their different ways. Not one face or foot or moo is like another's, though people just call them all 'cows.' Maisie slow and gentle, and the younger ones gobbling up the grass impatiently as if it might suddenly run out at the next chew.

We all have our dreams and ways, don't we? I would like to have a ranch with a thousand head of cattle and hundreds of wild horses. Our hopes prepare us for the day ahead. Otherwise we wouldn't know what to do when we meet our hens or cows or neighbours. It would be like the first time we saw them and we wouldn't know what to say or do. When we do meet we talk about the weather, which gives us the choice of talking about everything or nothing. Sometimes I think the day has happened already before I wake up.

I always hear the herd when lying in bed in the morning. I sleep well enough, from dark to dawn, summer and winter. Like a bear. It's all the same to me, though I hear folk complaining how different the two seasons are. Of course they are. I know that. It's all light during the summer and the grass grows and the cows feed on it so well. The mile journey takes longer then, because they spend so much time enjoying the clover, munching away to their hearts' content. I don't hurry them. Why would I? We have all day long to circumnavigate the world. Whether a long sunny summer's day or s short stormy winter's one makes no difference. We spend it together.

I like that. Summer. Sometimes I stand around resting

my chin on my hand on my stick on the ground watching them eating up all that goodness. Buttercups and daisies and orchids and thistles. My mouth waters. They enjoy it so much. It's good to see them happy. I keep one good inbye field as green as I can until late autumn to fatten them up before market time. They look at it yearningly all year long, and when I open the gate around the Feast of the Assumption, they run in like little children unsure for a while where to start eating. Pudding Field, I call it, because it reminds me of myself as a child when Mum made the best pudding in the world, rhubarb crumble with custard, on Friday nights when I came home from school. After dinner she used to sit in the warm corner by the stove, eyes screwed up, pins in her mouth, sewing. She was forever patching up Grandfather's clothes, as well as her own tweed skirts and, once, she knitted me up a teddy bear from the remnants of Grandfather's old tweed jacket which had gone beyond repair. His head was a mix of blue and green, his body grey, one leg white and one leg black. I stuffed him with sheep's wool and she stitched him all together. I named him Patch.

In the winter, the mile journey is so different. I leave them to find the scraps of grass and drops of unfrozen water as I follow along. Maisie looks up at me now and again, as if to say, 'Donald, can we just go back home? Please? And it's not because I'm a coward. It's because I'm wise.'

But I don't let them. Not because I'm cruel, but because I love them. I suppose I love them more than anything else in the world. For what else is there to love? And what a word that is anyway. I never hear anyone use it, except the priest on Sunday when he speaks about it. It's easy then.

The herd need to learn that winter can be enjoyed as much as summer. That after we do our mile-long circuit in snow and wind and rain, the reward is lying in their warm byre while I sit by the fire with my tea. We've endured. We've done it and survived once more! And enjoyed it too! O, I know that takes a while to achieve, because at first it's really depressing, first thing in the morning, watching the wind and rain sweeping in horizontally from the north and knowing fine that sleet and hailstones will follow, and that it will be all dark and getting darker as the day goes on, but once I've put my long johns and semmit and long woollen socks and my everlasting moleskin trousers on I'm ready for anything. We don't wish the rain or the winter away. We just prepare for it, as we do for sun and summer. Fresh straw in the byre. Those holes in the wall filled in. Gates and loose things tied down. Extra peats in by the fire. But I tell you, none of these practical measures take as much strength as believing in our daily walk.

And they sense it. I can hear them sniffing and snorting out in the byre as if they too are putting on layers for the task ahead, though all they have is the thick hair God gave them, and the patience and endurance handed down to them in their mother's milk. And Angus the bull: what a fine specimen he's been, going at it with patience and diligence over these past ten years, as was another Angus before him and Angus and Angus and Angus back through the generations. We all look forward to his arrival every year. He comes from the Department of Agriculture farm in Aberdeenshire and he moves from village to village for a whole month.

So, we all stand there in the faint morning light. The herd lined up behind Maisie who always leads and is standing mournfully in the byre door as the rain pounds the sodden yard in front of her. In the summer the light is so bright it blinds us. In the winter it's so dark we see everything, since we look so carefully. I once had an outbreak of rats in the barn but I made an *aoir* (a satire) telling them to go north and they did, because a curse, like a blessing, has infinite power. They never came back.

I no longer use a stick. In the early days, after my grandfather died and I was on my own with the cows, I did. To guide and goad and push them along, but I always felt it was wrong. And they knew it: looking at me sadly whenever I hit them on the rump or prodded the stirk in front.

'Good God. What a brute. A savage. Doesn't he know we know?' they all cried.

So gradually I gave the beatings up and replaced them with nods and hand-slaps and curses and words of rebuke and encouragement. They liked that. You have to let folk know how you feel, one way or the other. They like when my hand comes hard down on their back urging them on. The touch. Or the 'Hoi' I shout when one steps out of line, or the look I give when one barges the other. The one who had barged always looks at me then, like a sorry child. So I forgive.

'The herd will forgive you as you forgive them,' Grandfather said.

But especially they like it when I sing. I never used to because I always believed that was a woman's business. My mother was a wonderful singer. She had an endless number of songs, and though her voice wasn't that tuneful, or strong, the contents of the songs made up for everything. I only ever understood half of them when I was younger and still don't understand them all, though I've remembered them and sing them myself now when I'm out on the moor and the mood strikes me.

For it has to strike you. Not like a bolt of lightning, which will kill you, but like a soft breath of wind from the west, which keeps the midges and clegs and flies away on a good summer's day. You can hardly feel it at first, though I know the signs: the way the rushes in the river begin to bend ever so slightly, and that distant sort of hum in the air as if an oven or a door had been opened and a bit of warmth let out. Then you can feel the wind itself, as it floats across the machair and the cattle turn their heads that way, glad to be alive in the breeze.

The song thing is like that. It can happen any time. Say if I'm down on the machair digging the rigs where I'll plant the potatoes next spring, and I hit a stone or some obstacle in the ground and it makes me think of how Bonnie Prince Charlie also met with so much opposition on his way to London. Even Clanranald himself, my chief, telling him to go home that wonderful day he arrived in Eriskay, having sailed all the way from France. What a thing to say to the heroic prince, who was setting the plough fair for his people. What a harvest they could have had.

Or poor Seasaidh Bhaile Raghnaill and her family's opposition to her love for Dòmhnall, and how they eloped through a window and sailed for Australia. Sometimes I sing her song when milking the cows and I swear in the name of God that the milk flows sweeter and creamier when I do, because the cows are so happy that Seasaidh and Dòmhnall lived happily ever after. The only purpose of a song is to do something practical like make him fall in love with her or increase the creaminess of a cow's milk. Otherwise there's no point in singing it.

The thing is that the cows now look after themselves. They always have, in a way, because cattle and sheep can naturally sense where good grass lies and where fresh water is and where danger lurks, but I suppose through the generations they've also learned that. Genetically, I mean, because all that knowledge passes down from cow to calf, from mother to daughter, so that as each calf is born, he or she already knows the way, the mile. It's like a song. If a mother sings her daughter a song and she sings it to hers and so on, it only takes thirty of them to sing it before you're back a thousand years ago. I suppose they bring their own histories.

I sell the young bulls and heifers to MacTavish who comes round every year at Martinmas. The stock is kept clean from the Aberdeenshire Anguses.

I've had to learn it though. This mile I circumnavigate every day. I know every blade of grass and where every pebble and little stone lies and where the stream runs weak and strong and where the poisonous plants are. Nothing is hidden on it. I could walk it blindfold and know by the smell of the air and the contour of the ground where exactly I am. It's the one thing that's certain in our lives. And yet so much changes every day. See – that mark the hailstones made on the grass overnight, and the way the standing stone is damp this morning. The only way to see a thing is by looking at it so well you can see what you don't expect to see.

And here's the thing. You have to see everything before you see a single thing. When I go out in the morning I see the sky and the hills and the moor before I see anything else. It takes me a while to realise that's a heron standing stock still in the pond and – look – there's a robin sitting on the fencepost at the north end of the byre. I don't wear spectacles, so it's not a matter of focus. Just that I don't see anything until I've first of all seen everything. Though I know first thing in the morning the kind of day it will be by the sound it makes – that quiet hum that signifies peace and the equally quiet rumble that tells of coming turmoil.

The big advantage of walking the same mile every day is that it saves me choosing every morning and worrying every night about whether I made the right decision. If I started that carry-on there would be no end to it. West, down by the shore, or east directly towards the moor, or north beyond the big river or south towards the peatlands of Smiurasaraidh. And, of course, a hundred variations in between. How on earth could I then decide, except maybe by the direction of the prevailing wind, or the increasing weight of the clouds to the north south east or west, or the heights of the sea and the rivers after the rain or the spring and neap tides? Doing the one circuit saves all that thinking for better things. So Maisie and the herd and Rover and I just take things as they are, whatever direction the wind is coming from, wherever the clouds are, however fast or slow the river runs or how high or low the sea rises or falls.

But I don't suppose anyone else now knows or hears or sees all those things which call and chum me on my way round each day. Nurse MacLeish says it's just my memory and imagination, and she may be right. The old people used to believe that memory was a fairy gift. I don't have what they call 'second sight': that gift, or curse, of seeing the future. It's just first sight. I see everything around me shaped by the past, hanging around like a constant fog blanketing the future. It's like watching a film you've seen before. Or going to Mass. You know what's going to happen, but that's not why you go. The important thing is what could happen. The future might be different from the past. You never know. It gives you hope. The world will change because of these women saying the rosary.

It takes a while every morning to cast off the night. That rock was there yesterday, is it the same today? No, Donald, it isn't. See – the dew is still on it this morning, and that wasn't the case yesterday. And there's a bird. A lapwing standing in the reeds by the edge of the bog. She wasn't there yesterday. And up there – look – at the sky, the shape of the clouds this morning, light and fluffy, drifting slowly from south to west. They were all dark and brooding, hanging to the east yesterday. There's a thin cloud in the shape of a boat. That's Noah's Ark.

Even I'm different, having slept well again and had my breakfast of porridge and cream. 'Right Maisie,' I say. 'Off we go.'

And off she trots with her children, while I follow.

The round mile is a big wide open space. My neighbours say I just wander about in endless circles, but it's not like that at all. They've forgotten that the circle, not the arrow, was always our people's measure of time. The best thing about it is that you're forever making your way back to the beginning. The big space allows room for God. Our eyes are so limited. Hills and moor and sea and sheep and cows and people driving by, as if that's all there is. Maisie and the herd would be different if they weren't here. If they were corralled in big steel sheds or had all the green pastures of England to eat. They are the shape of the land here, lean and hardy. When I was wee, I believed people became their prayers. All those bent-over old women walking with their rosaries, and the stiff-backed men kneeling with their eyes closed. Arthur MacLennan, the salmon fisherman, grew scales on the back of his hands, and when Agnes MacRae – who cycled everywhere – prayed, her feet gently turned the pedals and then relaxed as she freewheeled down the brae.

The world changes as the day goes on. In the morning, everything is soft and fluffy, like a newborn lamb, and a wee bit unsure of what shape it is or ought to be. By noon all the rocks and streams and fences and gates and walls and houses stand out clear, proud in their certainty, but by evening begin to dissolve again into next to nothingness so that sometimes by the time I get back home in the winter dark I'm not sure if that wall is high or low, complete or broken. I only know through memory, which guides us all home, Maisie and the herd leading, with me following, and dear old Rover at heel.

2

MAISIE AND THE herd and I stop at the big rock after 224 yards. That's the first stop. There's good grazing there on all sides, but especially on the west and south sides. I rest against the rock, looking out towards the sea. The rock has a hollow where I can rest my back while fully stretching out my legs, and above the hollow is a narrow cleft where you can see things. Even rocks have insides. I think something is hidden inside everything.

You have to stand to look into it, and at first you don't see anything because it's all dark, but your eyes become accustomed to the darkness, or maybe the darkness becomes accustomed to you, I'm not sure which. After a while you can see in deeper and deeper, and the light gets brighter and brighter, and the shadows move and dance. It always surprises me that though the rock outside is grey, it's filled with all the colours of heaven inside: blue and green and mauve and red and orange and yellow and white and purple and lemon and others that I have no name for. Every time I look I see a different vision. I think they're pictures from stories I heard and read when I was a child, when stories were all that existed.

The other day it was a thousand ships with their red and white sails unfurled, all riding the waves as they sailed west, with dolphins and porpoises and sharks dancing and rising and plunging all around them, and yesterday it was a world of ice where Maisie and Rover and the herd and I were skating across the mountains, doing turns and twirls and leaps, and today it was a big thatched castle with turrets and flags of every colour flying and then the Chief came out wearing a flowing red robe, standing on his speckled horse with everyone waving and cheering, and then the warriors all climbed onto their smaller horses and leapt the high walls and, led by the Chief, galloped across this huge green field and on to the shore where the sand runs for miles and miles. The Chief was put on a galley with twelve oarsmen while the warriors and their wives and children ran and played and jousted on the sand all day long. The oarsmen sang a song I couldn't make out, rowing westwards. I could tell of thousands of things I've seen in that cleft, and they'd all be true.

My grandfather had horses, though they were nothing like these. Just four small Eriskay ponies used to pull his cart, and a big Clydesdale horse which did all the ploughing for him. Proper horses. Unshod.

'They're not children to dress up in shining shoes for school or church,' he said.

I spent a lot of time with Grandfather at the smithy. He went there to get the plough shares and coulters sharpened, or to get a new spade-head or new wheels for his cart. What a beautiful cart it was. He made it himself and allowed me to paint it, blue and red and yellow and orange stripes like I'd seen in the picture books. Old MacInnes the blacksmith was a deaf mute, but made up for it with his hands, melting iron like butter and turning out spades and knives and hammers and sickles that spoke and sang as they emerged out of the fire. I'm always surprised when a fire lights. First the smoke, then the white and red flames, as if God is saying, 'See, Donald. Everything's possible.' possible.' Moments before, there was nothing, and then suddenly – or sometimes after a struggle – there's smoke and flames and warmth. As long as something's possible it's bound to happen sometime.

Grandfather died when I was five. I don't remember the four small ponies, I do remember the Clydesdale. I suppose because he was so big. But when I really think about it, it's not the height or the bigness I remember but the smell. You don't smell it now because nobody has a horse like that anymore. It was a sort of strong sleepy smell, which I sometimes get a hint of when I rest at the tenth stop of the round mile and have a nap after lunch in the early afternoon. There's some wild garlic there, and it may be that, but it's also more – someone breathing a woman's perfume ever so faintly. The perfume my mother had when I was a baby.

The important thing about this rock is not really the cleft but the fissure on the west side where *Mac Talla nan Creag* lives. In English that means The Son of the Echo of the Hall of the Fissure of the Rocks. He has a long genealogy, like everyone else here had once upon a time. Though I call him Dòmhnall. Donald. The same name as myself. Unlike everyone in the cleft, you never see him, because he's just a voice, and if you call out to him, he always answers, because he must get quite lonely living all by himself far inside that rock. So I always speak to him. When I speak wee (in a whisper), he replies wee, and when I speak loud, he speaks back loud. But you must speak slowly, for if you speak fast the words get lost in the rock and become mere sounds, which not even *Mac Talla nan Creag* can untangle.

'Hallo!' I shout, and there's always a delay before he replies, and it's always the sound of my own voice that comes back to me, as if he's become so used to my voice that he's become me. Maybe all we ever hear is our own voice anyway. I speak to him in Gaelic.

'*Ciamar a tha thu an-diugh?*' ('How are you today?') I shout, and instead of answering 'Fine' or something plain like that, he just asks me back the same question, '*Ciamar a tha thu an-diugh?*' His voice echoes and rebounds as if he's not one but two or three people.

'*Gle mhath*' ('Very well'), I call back, and he says he's the same, and then I always ask him, '*Dè tha dol an-diugh ma-thà?*' ('What's doing today then?'), and he's so civil and kind and respectful and asks me the same question back. I say '*Och, direach a' buachailleachd mar as àbhaist*' ('Och, just herding as usual'), and he says he's doing the same thing and I ask him how he's getting on and he asks me and I say fine and he says fine too and we talk about the weather for a while, though some days, when the weather is fine and sunny and you can hear forever, we talk about greater things such as the plummeting price of cattle and the terrible ways the supermarkets are taking all the profits, leaving us poor herdsmen on the edge of poverty. We then say goodbye, '*Bruidhnidh mi leat a-màireach ma-thà*' ('I'll speak to you tomorrow then'), and he promises the same and of course we do, day after blessed day, because he never lets me down, never has, unlike some of the folk around here who never speak to me or answer me or answer with rubbishy promises that they never fulfil. Everyone I know is so broken that they can't speak any more.

They say *Mac Talla nan Creag* was the eldest son of the High King in the olden days, but he was spoilt and demanded everything for himself. He was selfish and huffy and refused to speak to anyone, because he thought they were not worthy of speaking to him. So the people rose up against him and took hold of him and put him inside the rock until he learned to listen properly and know how important people's names and stories are. So he listens and calls back the exact story you tell him, and once he's listened to everything everyone has to say he can come out and tell his own story. After I speak to him, I always put my ear to the rock to find out if he's saying anything for himself, but it's always silent. What a story he'll have though, when he's set free.

The thing is you can't trust folk. Forever saying one thing and doing another. And forever looking away. Talking only of things they've heard on the radio or seen on television or read in the paper. Things I know already. Never about themselves, or what they think or feel. They think I'm strange. I know that. Sense it in the way they move. The Last of the Mohicans, wandering about here in this eternal circle every day while they go about their business in fancy cars, speeding along the road as if time is running out. Time! Every day is like the blink of an eye and like an eternity. Maisie after Maisie after Maisie across the years, and every morning there she is with her calm eyes waiting for me to open the byre door so she can go off to eat more grass. And she eats each blade of grass as if it were the first ever blade of grass, believing that the grass will never end. that the grass will never end. For when one mouthful finishes, another begins. It's always the end of something, and the beginning of something else.

'What do you think, Maisie?' She turns towards me. She's such an honest creature, unwilling to lie. She trusts me, like a child trusting a good father. I wonder if she suspects how fragile I am. I think she does. Otherwise she wouldn't be so kind and gentle with me, looking at me with those big brown sad eyes.

I believe with her, and so the day becomes one long slow day for me too. As there is grass, there will be pebbles and stones and the stream and the loch and *Lòn a' Phùinnsein* and the Fairy Hollow and Mary Ann and Catrìona and Eòghainn and Mr Haas, permanently absent from his big beautiful empty house. Maisie and the herd and I walk so slowly that sometimes we pass ourselves from twenty or thirty or three hundred years ago, walking and grazing these same fields with our ancestors. For moments, I can be someone else. *Mac Talla nan Creag* or Eòghainn, newly returned from overseas and running to find Catrìona waiting at the window, or the teller of a long story instead of a mere cowherd. I see what I believe.

O, I hear them talking all right. '*Às a chiall*' ('mad'). '*An truaghan*' ('poor soul'). I know they pity and feel sorry for me and despise me too, in part because I'm not up to date and stubbornly keep to my old ways. And my socks and wellingtons smell, like that's a judgement on our community. Letting them all down. By the way, my wellington boots feel too big for me these days. Maybe I'm getting smaller in my old age. I was once 33, which is the perfect age.

What a word that is anyway – community. I hear it all over the place now, on Gaelic radio and in the local paper when they talk about these endless meetings they're having. Community this and community that and community the other, as if we're all in the same peatbog together, when most aren't, since they have oil central heating.

Maybe I just like the place rather than the people. What if the cows and sheep and the rocks and grass and the stream and heather and that changeable sky above and the little hillocks where the fairies live are my neighbours? My community. For who's to say that Archie and Janet and Faye down the road make this place any more than Maisie or Rover or my cat Wilhelmina does? Wilhelmina who lies there purring on my knees every night, and Rover who greets me every morning with a lick on my face and chums me all day long with the cows, and

Maisie whose sense knows no bounds.

'*Dè do bheachd, Maisie?*' ('What do you think, Maisie?') I keep asking her, and she turns her big brown eyes towards me. It saves both of us from indifference.

I'd be dead if it weren't for Maisie. Maybe I had a dram too many that night, but when I went to bed I left the guard off the fire and the peats must have spilled out and burnt the rug and there was me snoring away until I heard Maisie mooing for dear life down by the scullery door, so of course I woke all worried about her and immediately smelt the burning and rushed down in my underwear to find everything around the fire in flames. I was a strong man then. I lifted the big water barrel outside the door with my bare hands and emptied it over the fire, and O, how Maisie and the herd following her enjoyed the sauna steam that rose and flowed through the house, warming them on a cold and frosty night.

I led them out and fed them from the special hoard of oats I keep for weaning them, and the feed must have reminded them all of their childhoods, because as soon as they started eating it they all began to behave like babies. The memory they had of trusting their mothers when they were young.

They are my family. The ones I look to for support and sustenance. They matter to me. They are my livelihood, of course, for how else would I live if not for my herd of cows. The annual sale keeps me in essentials all winter and through early spring while the milk and crowdie and cheese they give me fills my table, and their meat in the freezer sustains me. I kept on Mum's hens and sheep after she died, but I never cared for them as much as for the cows. I've now made an arrangement with Janet Smith who cares for them and gives me eggs and wool and mutton in exchange for my prime beef. Occasionally I shoot a duck or cormorant for a different taste. Their bones make good soup.

3

WE STOP AT the old peat banks, where I kissed Mary Ann. They were long hot summer days then, and she was home on holidays from Glasgow. We'd spent the week turning the peats so that the other side would dry, and I don't suppose we laboured that much because we were young and just helping the adults who did most of the work. We could have spent the rest of our lives out on the moor, brown and young together.

I'd turn half a dozen peats or so, and Mary Ann worked with me, because her parents said she didn't know anything about peats and would learn from me. I showed her how to lift them and how to turn them and where to place them, and that was really all there was to it. Bending down towards the earth and picking up what was there and placing it the other way round.

Most of the time we played. *Falach-fead*: hide-and-seek or hide-and-whistle as we called it. She'd hide and I'd whistle a tune, and at the end of the tune I went looking for her and after I found her it was her turn and she said she didn't know how to whistle so I taught her the shepherd's trick of the pinkie and forefinger in the side of the mouth and then a big long whistle, which of course wasn't the same as whistling a pipe tune or something like that, but it was fine because it distinguished the two of us, with the grown-ups knowing I whistled tunes and that Mary Ann whistled like a shepherd calling her dogs.

'It's nice to sit on the grass,' she said.

That day we were resting behind one of the small peat stacks. Winter takes its toll, with frost and ice and rain, and by spring the bogland is what it is: a bog. But then, bit by bit, it dries out. The wind gets warmer and there's a bit of sun and the pools of water diminish and the rivulets thin out and by Easter time it's ready for turfing – removing the top clods of earth. And then let things dry and when May comes, out with the *trèisgear* to the cut the peats, one wet slice at a time, and best to have a pal to work with, one cutting and one flinging, but I usually do it myself now, cutting a yard or two, then flinging, then cutting and flinging. And then you leave these to dry through May and June and sometimes July, turning them once a week or so, until both sides are crisp and dried before taking them home in those heavenly days of August when the bog cotton blows in the breeze and everything is as it was when you were a child, but you sense that behind it all is the coming of colder days and the long winter nights when the work you've done all summer long will be rewarded as you sit there warming up by the fire you cut and lifted yourself on a long ago May morning.

We were at that turning time when Mary Ann and I

sat behind the stacks. Some of the peats had dried enough to make into small stacks to be gathered together into bigger ones later on, and they gave shelter and extra warmth as we sat there in the summer sun. We were playing 'Soldiers' – knocking the heads of the *slàn-lus* (the ribwort plantain) — and Mary Ann was well ahead. And then she turned and kissed me, because I'm sure it was not I who turned and kissed her, though it may just have been the two of us at the same time, for something else to do, and it was ever so strange and soft and sweet like when I was wee I brushed against my Mum's soft jersey when she washed my hair in the sink in the kitchen and she smelt of the lavender flowers she gathered and kept in a glass jar by her bed. She always asked me to gather some on the way back home from school for her, and she had a locket with a pressed flower inside it she wore to church every Sunday. Her favourite colours was yellow and blue, and every year when the daffodils and irises come into bloom I see her picking a handful of each to brighten up the window sills.

Mary Ann's kiss was a summer kiss, which I learned later on was so different from the hard winter kisses the grown-ups did down at the dances in the hall when they'd stand out in the biting wind in the dark, the men fighting their way into the poor girl's arms, driven by the desire to be near some comfort and warmth, some other human being, away from the cold and the coming snow and the loneliness. What did the past or future matter at that wild moment?

When she touched my lips with hers it was as if a

butterfly had touched me and gone. I watched them often down on the machair, flitting from orchid to poppy, from buttercup to clover. Moments here and moments there, as if they had all the time in the world to taste every flower for miles and miles.

Hovering over this one, coming to rest on another, and I'm always astonished how weightless they seem, making no mark where they've landed to feed. Unlike me, squelching through the mud every other day in my big boots, crushing the earth with every step I take. One step always carries us towards the next, and on and on we go. When my mother realised she'd made a mistake in her knitting, she'd ripple out the stitches back to where the fault was and start all over again. Could I do that now, at my age?

Mary Ann's kiss was the first tender moment of my life beyond my mother, and when I sit here every day by the peat banks, now overgrown because everyone has oil, I think of her. Of the two of them and how kind they were. Every time I came home from school I could smell Mum's cooking from outside the garden wall: broths and stews and – every Friday – fish. And she'd be standing there in her apron, covered with flour, forever making scones that I covered with butter and jam.

Mary Ann had a dress with blue flowers on that day, and her bare legs and knees were black with peat stains. I'd told her just to bend over to lift the peats but she insisted on doing it on her knees, so she had no one to blame but herself. Said it was more comfortable.

'Anyway,' she said, 'I like best squelching through

that mud in the lower side of the bog. That's proper fun.'

I must have fainted when she kissed me, because I have no recollection of what happened between the butterfly touch and us standing up and looking around to make sure no one had seen us. Her parents were far away up the hill gathering the sheep.

It was the best day of my life, and I'll tell you why: it was the day I learned that one butterfly kiss is worth more than a thousand head of cattle. As I trudge here through long cold bleak winters herding my cows backwards and forwards, sometimes through the mud and sometimes under the blazing sun, that time comes to me again and again, telling me that I should have asked her to marry me there and then and run away with her to the mainland and become a shepherd on the rolling hills of Perthshire or an auctioneer in Aberdeenshire or a factory worker in Glasgow instead of this miserable life I lead. Me and my poor cows. For when I say I have a herd it means I have seven cows: Maisie and her offspring. They're not a herd, they're individual cows. Maisie and Bellag and Curstag and Tomaidh and Sòbhrag and Mòrag and Susag, each with his and her own way, the way they walk and limp and graze and look at me. Susag, for example, always does what she's told, whereas Bellag pauses for a moment, and then does what she wants. They know if you're cheating. Just herding them or feeding them because you have to. They're ashamed of me then.

Mary Ann would have said yes, and yes again. I know it. Because she said as much to me when I asked her about it years and years later. We met out at the pier while she was home for a holiday with her husband and children.

But it was not to be. I carry it with me and try to forget all about it except when I sit here each morning at the disused peat banks knowing what could have been, and never will be again. Where else will I meet a woman, unless I advertise in the paper, which would shame me to death. No women come out here on the moor anymore. And it's too late now anyway, at my age. I have no one to cuddle up to in bed, though I like the big space it gives me to stretch out any way I want. But I never do that. I always lie on the wall side of the bed, which I can lean against in the dark. Wilhelmina lies at my feet, waiting to shame me if I move and disturb her. I shamed myself the last time I went to a dance when I said to Morag as we separated after the waltz, 'You're a lovely sheaf of a woman,' and she said I was daft and hurried away.

There used to be lots of weddings here. For days before, the boys carousing and the girls preparing and then the day of the marriage, the bride in white sitting high on a cart with Smith the cobbler steering the horse (though later on, after he died, the brides travelled on the trailer of his son's tractor) up the brae to the church and the sung Mass as the sun shone through the high stained glass window where Christ the Shepherd cared for his flock, and then the dinner in the church hall, hens that the women had plucked and prepared, and the 'dainties' Mum was so fond of and brought home in little cardboard boxes to send to relatives in Australia and Canada. Now couples just live together without any of that ritual or joy or ceremony. I miss the life of it.

I have my tender moments still, though. *Coinean*, the wee teddy rabbit I had as a child and which I dumped when I became a man. But I found him again some years ago, covered in muck and dust and cobwebs and ash in the back of the scullery cupboard the day I cleared and cleaned it out after the fire. The one ear and that daft lop-sided smile of his that says he knows I'm still a child.

So I took him and washed him all clean with soap suds and hung him out to dry on the line and he swung there for weeks with his sideways smile until one night the frost came and there he was all frozen and shivering in the morning so I took him in by the fire where he thawed out and rested and now he's my best friend, because Maisie is not allowed into the house. He's a bit ragged and patched now but as soft and kind as he ever was.

'There you are,' I say to him when I return from my daily herding, 'Missed me, eh?'

'Of course,' he says, smiling that lop-sided smile of his. 'And how was your day, Donald?'

'Och. So, so,' I say. 'Same old, same old. Round and round the magic circle as they say.'

And then I make a mug of tea for myself, and I know by the way he looks at me that he too would like a cup, so I take out the little china cup my mother used on special occasions and fill it with water and give him the side dish of fresh grass I plucked on my round, and he sits there gurgling and clucking away, happy that I've made it home again, that the fire is on and that Maisie and all the herd are humming away in the warm barn at the end of the house, resting in the soft hay. I watch the changing shapes of the flames in the fire, sometimes thick and grey like winter clouds, sometimes light and blue like a summer's day. I learned 'Hiawatha' at school. On winter nights I tell it to myself and Coinean and Wilhelmina and Rover by the fire, and when I tell it I'm not just remembering or saying the words. I become Hiawatha. It's good to be someone else for a while. I learn of every bird its language and all their names and secrets, how they build their nests in summer, where they hide themselves in winter, and how the beavers built their lodges and where the squirrels hid their acorns and how the reindeer ran so swiftly and why the rabbit was so timid and all those things we used to tell one another. But only professionals do it now when they come round with their shows to the community centre. Nobody whistles any more, either when they're working or walking along, so sometimes I do Whistling Rufus after Hiawatha. But I do have a whistling kettle, which breaks the silence when it boils.

'Take care of the weakest calf in the herd,' Mum said, 'and then the whole herd will love you.'

I cry then, for otherwise I would take down the whisky bottle I keep for Hogmanay.

4

THE KIND OF morning it is makes no difference to me. Snow, hail, rain or shine, I open my eyes at the first light, when the sun rises. It's the day's best hour. My bedroom upstairs faces east so even in my sleep I can sense that faint grey-orange glow in the sky well before the sun itself rises. I wonder if it's like me in the summertime and has to throw its blankets off to sleep comfortably?

I open my eyes when the sun opens his, and I lie for a while listening to the sounds of the waking morning. It's a sort of distant hum at first, like a swarm of bees on a summer's morning, except that it doesn't get any louder. It remains at that pitch like a slow Gaelic song. I don't think that hum ever goes – I think it's the world revolving on its axis – just that it is replaced, or overtaken, by other sounds which waken into the light.

I often wonder if I walked and kept walking eastwards with Maisie and the herd and Rover if we'd all walk into a perpetual sunrise? That must be the case, for if the sun rises in the east, then it must continue to rise there forever as you go towards it. But we'd probably have to travel very fast to keep up with it, which of course is impossible with Maisie and the herd who like to stop and taste every blade of grass on the way. Rover could do it because he can run faster than anyone or anything else I know, though he'd get tired and need to rest every mile or so. No one can keep going forever.

'What do you think, Maisie?'

The cockerel crows and Rover barks and Wilhelmina purrs. I hear distant rumbles and tumbles as various neighbours begin to go about their business. But the best sound is my mother's voice in the kitchen calling upstairs, 'Donald. It's time.' And I climb out of bed and wash and dress and down the stairs I go, and she must have gone out for her walk again for the place is empty, though with that whiff of mint perfume she leaves every morning, and I stir the porridge I left soaking in the pan overnight and fling in a thimbleful of salt and by the time that's ready I've stoked and resurrected the fire and I can already hear Maisie mooing in the byre waiting for me and the day's long adventure.

'Come on then. Let's do it.'

We do the first and the second stop again and then reach the hollow where the fairies live. I've gone full circle and beyond. When I was a child, older people talked about them and I believed them. When I became a man, I thought that they'd made it all up, but now that I'm that age, and know my own fears and hopes and dreams, they are more real than ever, living away there in the knoll as they always were. I hear them dancing and singing under the knoll when we stop there. I'm sure they do it so we can hear them. Maisie lifts her head like she too is hearing them, but then just shakes her horns as if some flies had buzzed about her ears and gets on with grazing. She wanders over to the left where the sweetest grass lies, and the herd all follow. I stand with my chin on my hands resting on the stick watching them all. My grandfather told me that all good children before they were ready for heaven went to the fairy knoll first, to play for a thousand years without having to do any chores like cutting the hay or taking the water in.

I wonder if they'll play 'Fling the Chuckie in the Bunnet' in heaven? That was the game I liked best at school, though we called it *Bonaidean* (Bonnets) at the time. I don't suppose they play it now because the children don't wear bonnets to school. They probably use something else like an empty tin now instead of a bonnet. We threw our bonnets as far as we could and the one who threw it furthest then got the first chance to throw a marble into it. Seonaidh Smith always had them in his bag. The one who landed the most marbles in the furthest bonnet was King for the day.

Meantime we could hear the girls skipping and singing over in the other corner of the grass.

> '*Cha tèid mi laighe nochd gus am faigh mi rudeigin*
> *Rudeigin, rudeigin.*
> *Cha tèid mi laighe gus am faigh mi na trì casan*
>   *caorach*
> *Trì casan, trì casan, trì casan caorach.*
> *Trì casan agus broillean, trì casan caorach.*

Trì casan agus broillean agus pìos den mhaoidheil,
'S cha tèid mi laighe nochd gus am faigh mi rudeigin.'

('I will not go to bed tonight until I get something to eat
Something, something.
I will not lie down until I get three sheep's feet.
Three feet, three feet, three sheep's feet,
Three feet and a breast, three sheep's feet,
Three feet and a breast and a piece of the paunch,
And I shall not go to bed tonight until I get something to eat.')

And then big Bessie MacTavish, who had learned a bit of English schoolyard songs and rhymes and chants from a distant cousin who lived in Fort William, always sang,

'Hallelujah make a dumpling
Hallelujah bring it ben
Hallelujah make a big one
Hallelujah amen.'

And they would all shout out that last line.

There are no children in the village now. When I was young, there were over a hundred in the primary school, but that closed years ago. I was an only child, because my father died before I was in the cradle, but most other houses had six, seven or eight children. They've all gone away, and their houses are now empty all winter, but occupied by older couples from the mainland during the summer. I miss the sound of children playing, especially on those May mornings when the cuckoo calls and the larks and peewits and curlews are singing and crying their hearts out. Mary Ann and I used to look for their eggs. Our favourite ones were the peewit and plover eggs, with their beautiful speckled spots. We'd just look at them, because it was wrong to remove them. We could hear their mothers crying until we left, running across the machair, being birds. Mary Ann was an oystercatcher and I was a seagull.

I do a lot of standing during the day, which may be why I stayed slim after all these years. I stand with my hands resting on the stick because all the weight then goes onto the hazel wood and from there into the ground and even if I stand like that for an hour or two I don't feel stiff or anything, and can then move on as light as a feather because all the gravity has gone down into the earth. I wish I could stand without a stick, but I can't. Not that I would stumble or fall down, but that I would feel unfinished, like a tree without a branch, or a bird without a song. Strange that gravity doesn't affect birds, who can soar off no matter how heavy the earth is. I suppose God gave them that special gift, which cows don't have either. They'd be too heavy, I guess, even if they had wings.

I've had so many sticks over the years. Hazel, oak, birch, chestnut, tall, thin, long, short and stubby, but these were all bought from merchants at the annual sales. I carve the real thing myself, which is difficult in this place with hardly any trees. I rely on *faodail* – treasures – from the shore. Odds and ends and bits and pieces brought in by the tide. The bench by my fire is a slab of oak left after a winter storm, but a big bit like that is very rare.

Mostly it's rubbish – plastic bottles and such stuff, but now and again an oar or a plank of wood or a fine bit of carpentry drifts in which I can shape into anything I want with my chisel and scalpel and gouge. My prize possession is a sailor's chest, with magnificent carvings of elephants and tigers and leopards down the side, that sailed in on the tide one day. I keep my winter blankets in there.

As I stand, resting on my stick, the cattle do their business. Stop and graze and piss and let their dung go, and I suppose that's what keeps this hollow so nice and fresh and green. You couldn't get better fertilizer anywhere in the whole world, though I confess that the horses were even better for the land when we had them. In my grandfather's day the grass was greener and richer because of them. That big Clydesdale. He had could have manured the whole of Egypt by himself.

'Never hit a horse on the head,' he said. 'It's where their spirit lives.'

I'm proud of this land. This bare and rocky place. I've helped to make it what it is: able to withstand anything. I'm also proud of my barrow. It's lasted me my whole life. Others replace theirs every ten years or so because a wheel has fallen off or because it's been left out in the rain to rot and decay. They haven't taken enough care of it. It's the most useful thing I have. I use it first thing every morning for mucking out the byre and then all through the year for every essential job, from carrying the peats home to moving stones and carrying sacks of flour. I don't know what I'd do without Rover and my barrow. He's such a good and faithful dog. I've only ever had one bad dog, a long time ago. Lazy and unwilling to work in the rain. The worse was I knew fine that, just as easily, he could have been good and willing. I gave him away to a traveller at the annual fair. Claimed he could train him. Bought an experienced collie from MacPherson the auctioneer. Thing is, you don't need to train a dog if you have an old dog around. Every time Rover gets old I get a young collie and the old one teaches him all the wisdom of dogs.

The part of the hollow where the fairies live lies untouched by my herd. The cattle don't go into it, and not because of any spooky reason – just that there's quite a sharp incline which they find hard to climb and then an equally difficult descent on the other side into the hollow itself. They could do it if they wanted, but I don't think they can be bothered, though the sheep are there in their dozens and rabbits in their hundreds. While the cattle graze I climb into it and lie on my back on the higher incline, because from there I can still see the herd. The world is more than I can see. I suppose the fairy hill is the place where we are and where we are not, like the way on a clear winter's night I feel I could reach right up into the sky and pluck the moon down to earth, but don't try because I want it to remain a possibility, and not something I tried and failed to do.

Some say the fairies are fallen angels, others that they're the spirits of our ancestors. Some say they turn to dust if touched. Others that it's the other way round, and that it's us who become ashes. Some say they're good, and others say they're bad. I don't know. I don't think I'd be any better off if I knew everything. All that matters is that they're here, same as we are.

The grass is soft as a bed and if folk wouldn't talk about it I'd be inclined to sleep there forever. But they would. I know already what they call me. *An Gloic* (The Idiot), although some are kinder and just call me *An t-Amadan* (The Fool). I don't really know what the difference is, except I sense that calling me an idiot has something to do with my brain and calling me a fool just to do with my ways. And, I tell you, there's nothing wrong with my brain. Or with my ways, if it comes to that. Maybe it's their ways and brains that are strange.

I left school at 14, so I don't know a lot, except about cows and sheep and grass and hay and seaweed and things which seem increasingly irrelevant here these days. Why would anyone bother with them when they can get their sausages and chops and potatoes and carrots from the shop down the road without getting their hands dirty? My grandfather kept his cows in the other end of the house, but since then they've been exiled outside, to the byre. Only cats and dogs are now allowed inside houses.

I'm all dirt. How couldn't I be, working all day with animals? Constantly covered in rain and wet and slime and mud while the world has gone all clean and antiseptic, as if milk didn't come from udders, and pork from pigs which were yesterday rolling in the mud, and as if lettuce and onions and shallots had been grown in plastic bags, and maybe they are now for all I know. Even though I wash my hands morning and night the grain of earth still lies in them unmoved. I don't chew my nails, so everyone can see the wee bits of mud under them, despite all my efforts. Small seed potatoes might grow from my skin if I live long enough. I hope so.

I suppose that's what makes this green and pleasant hollow such a sacred place for me. It's the one place where there's no cow dung. O, I know there are thousands of sheep and rabbit pellets, but these are nothing. Just small dry round things, like peas. I lie there in the soft green grass, and I don't hear the little fairies at first, probably because I've disturbed them and they've gone all quiet the way you do when a stranger appears and you wonder whether he's safe. The old people used to tell us to avoid the fairy knowes, especially in the dark, but ever since Mary Ann and I dared to walk through it after dusk and we stood there until we heard them singing and dancing, I've never been afraid of it. They were just like us, wanting to be happy. Maybe they wanted to be us and us to be them. All of us singing and dancing and playing together. They're not meant to chum us on the way to the shop or sit beside us on the bus on the way to the ferry and common things like that, but are here for special moments.

Even now, when they must be so used to the sound of

my boots on their roof, they still pause when I first arrive and settle down, and it's only when I've lain there on my back for five minutes or so that they begin to move, at first ever so quietly and then more and more daringly, the way you do when you know everything is safe, and as it was before. I must sound very heavy to them, because they don't really weigh anything, light as air.

They run around like children, because they are all forever young, I suppose. Although the folk who've seen them say some of them are old and wizened, so maybe they are just like us after all, with their hopes and fears, their ills and ailments. I hear little chuckles and giggles, the way we used to be in that first year in primary school before we settled into pecking orders, and you could only do things with the permission of the teacher or one of the class leaders.

They called me 'Wellies' at school because I always wore my wellington boots. There was no choice. I didn't have any other shoes except my Sunday ones and they'd be spoilt at school, and besides, if I wanted to wear them I wouldn't have time to put them on because I had to get up early and help mum with milking the cows and cleaning the byre before I went to school and by the time that was done I had to run there and wash my boots as best as I could in the river on the way. There's no bridge across the river, so we just waded across it. But you had to know where or you'd be swept away.

The river is called *Abhainn an t-Saighdear* (The Soldier's River). It would have had an older name, but that's now forgotten because of the soldier Alasdair Mòr

MacEacharna. He returned from the Battle of Balaclava with just one leg and one arm but could nevertheless swim across the river when it was in full flood. On rainy nights I can hear the river tumbling over the cliff pool where he eventually drowned.

Another boy in school was nicknamed 'Nose' because whenever anyone asked his father anything he'd always say, 'I don't know, but my son John knows.' The only thing I remember about Nose is that he always wondered where the numbers on the blackboard had gone when the teacher rubbed them out.

'They can't just have disappeared. They must have gone somewhere, for they were here a moment ago.'

So he'd inspect the duster after the class and shake his head because they weren't there either.

The worst thing we had to do at school was called 'Composition', when the teacher told us to write a story. 'What I did at the weekend', or 'What life will be like in 100 years' time.' How could anyone tell in a few words on a page what they'd done at the weekend, or what life might be like in 100 years' time? It would take forever and anyway it would be better told than written. Especially since we were instructed to write it in English, which for most of us was like asking a sheep to bark like a dog. But we've learned to bark all right. The school book stories were always teaching us something, without us knowing it. We thought they were just stories.

The river is my friend. It waters the land and the herd, and the way it then flows down the brae into the open sea is a delight to observe. It's like the way I pour a cup of tea from the pot. I've learned over the years how to do it properly. I can now pour the tea from the pot into any cup or dish or saucer from any height without spilling or splashing a single drop. It looks like the Niagara Falls when I do it. It's part of the reason why I never go to what they call social functions, because the lukewarm tea you get there is just dribbled into these tiny cups which are so far removed from the majesties of the river and the ocean. I remember my grandfather, when he lost his sight, sticking his thumb into the cup as he poured the tea to know it was full.

Seonaidh Mòr led us all in the playground and none of us could do much without his permission because he was the strongest lad in the class. I think it's like that down in the fairy knoll, because, just like us in school, after a while the chuckles and giggles stop, and I can hear a louder voice saying things while all the others are silent. I can't make out what he's saying.

I'm sometimes like that. When I go to the shop or any public place, the words I want to use come out of my mouth, but I can't work out what I'm saying. The words come out in dribs and drabs in a sort of haphazard way which makes little sense, while others speak as if they're pouring water into a glass and not spilling a single word. No wonder they call me an idiot and a fool. And yet exactly the same words make so much sense when I speak them in to myself or when I – sometimes – speak them out to myself by the fire. Then they make perfect sense. I believe in them then, yet when I speak them out to someone else they are like old ashes in the fire, a sort of nothingness.

But obviously the man's words down in the knoll aren't like that, for as soon as he finishes speaking, harps and bagpipes and drums and flutes and whistles and the sound of tirling erupt and the grass on which I lie begins to quiver and shake and Maisie and her herd glance up at the noise, and, seeing nothing, return to their grazing. Someone sings a song. It's a long slow Gaelic lament, and then the whole knoll takes up the chorus, filling the air with sorrow and sadness, but as soon as that's done someone strikes up a reel on the pipes and the earth shakes again with enjoyment.

I've searched and searched, but for the life of me can't find the entrance to this knoll. You can never find the door from the outside. They have to open it for you. You don't enter by chanting some magic word, such as Abracadabra, but by trusting them. It comes from custom and habit. They know who wants to play and who doesn't. Who believes and who doesn't. Magic wants things to happen without any hassle. Life is not like that. I have to feed and milk and look after the herd every day, and clean and muck the byre every night. Maybe that's the magic. The knoll sits there, and the little people work and play inside it, just as the sea is over to the west where the fish live and play in it under water and the loch to the east where the swans swim and the moor to the south where the sheep graze and the mountain on the other side, to the east. If a thing is there, it's there.

I know every blade of grass. It has remained unmoved for the past fifty years, constantly kept cropped by the sheep. They must have gone in ages and ages ago, well before my time, or else they must go in and out invisibly, like wisps of air or like these atoms Mr Morrison went on about in school. He demonstrated how atomic theory worked by blowing bubbles into the air until they popped and then saying, 'And that's how things disappear. Your task now is to find out where they went.'

Oh, I know fine there are accounts of folk getting into the knoll and dancing there for a hundred years and then emerging the same age they were, to find the world they once knew all changed and the earth people they knew as little children all dead and gone. I often feel like that when I lie in bed at night and everything is quiet and silent and I think of everyone I knew once upon a time. I can see them all as they were years and years ago when I was child, but when I wake in the morning they're gone, and all I can hear is Janet Smith and her hens cackling on the horizon. I'm sure Grandfather would weep if he were to come out of the knoll and see the state of things, with no horses or scythes or sheaves of corn. I only saw them once. It's the place where things are revealed to you.

I think the world has just become too strange for them. For if they were to come out, what would happen to them nowadays? Be run over by a car or a 4x4 or a tractor and be investigated by X-ray machines and technology and the media. Cameras everywhere catching and distorting the truth. So, it's no wonder they hide. I'm a patient man. One day the earth will open up and I will see them again and join them in their game for a hundred years and a day.

But what amazing grace that I can hear them. No one else around here can. For none of them spend the time out here that I do, forever rushing by in their cars and on their electric bikes. I'm the only one who's slow and spends every day out here, so I suppose they've accepted me into their community. Even if they pause every time they hear my big boots above their heads. It's always probably like the first time for them and then one of them says, 'Ach, don't worry. It's just Donald.' And then they restart their games and music and dancing and playing. You can't do any of that if you're worrying or thinking that people are tut-tutting because you're just playing and dancing instead of digging a ditch with a spade or working away on a computer.

When I'm lying there I join in whistling and singing all their tunes and seem to know them all, as if I've heard them all before and yet as if they are newly created, but as soon as I rise, all the tunes and the dance steps I knew so well vanish, no matter how hard I try to recapture the melody or the dance. If I could remember them just the once I would be the greatest musician and dancer in the world.

Instead, when I get up, my heavy boots are like lead. The songs that filled my heart as I lay there become cow words again, with the herd ever so attentive as I move them on again with a '*Shoo*' and a '*Siuthad*' and a '*Shush*' and other solitary instructions so far removed from those underground mumblings.

5

SOMETIMES THE COWS walk in a straight line, following Maisie, sometimes they don't. I like watching them walk. Left foreleg first and then the back right leg. Then the right front and the left back. A few inches at a time, constantly eating grass. They see or smell or sense something to the side and one wanders off, and as soon as one wanders the others follow. I don't corral them. It's their world more than mine. Unless they're tempted towards the dangerous bog after the fairy knoll.

It's the one place on the round mile which is deadly. We don't avoid or fear it but learn to make our way round it. Then it won't deceive us. When the weather is dry they're tempted to drink from there. The older ones know the algae is poisonous, but the young ones are always tempted to dip their heads into the water unless their mothers, or my stick, prevents them. It's like Cuchullin's sword stopping everything in its path. Every time I use a stick to lean on or to prod the herd I marvel that a bit of wood has become my strength and their guide.

Lòn a' Phùinnsein (The Poison Pool) they call the

bog here, for so many cattle have died over the years and so many folk have drowned, most making their way home from the pub on a dark winter's night. They say it's haunted, though it's only haunted by the guilt of their families and friends, who should have cared for them better when they were alive. If they'd been home they would never have drowned.

Shapes become other things in the dusk and dark. Past the turn of the night. A sheep becomes a bush and a familiar rock the devil himself waiting to pounce. They're probably like that during the day as well, except I don't notice or think about it. Day and night are so different. And not everyone sees what I see. Not because I'm special but because I know the history of the place. I suppose the ruins of a house are the ruins of a house unless Catrìona is standing there in the open window, waiting for us, when it's not the ruins of a house at all but a home where the kettle is on the boil, ready for the tea once the talking is done. Everything could just as easily be something else if we weren't used to it. Like Nose, I sometimes wonder where the light goes when the darkness comes.

This glen used to be known as *Gleann Ghoiridh* (Goiridh's Glen), though everyone now just calls it 'The Glen.' I suppose they've forgotten who Goiridh was. Grandfather told me he was a man from Canada who arrived here after the Napoleonic War and set up as an itinerant teacher. Taught not only French and Mathematics but also swordsmanship and archery, which died out when all the young men who'd learned how to use a sword and bow went away to war and died in the trenches where nothing but luck or fate could defend you. I'm the only one who uses these old names around here, if only to the herd and to Rover. Most of the other folk who live here go away to the mainland every second weekend, so I suppose one name is as good as another to them.

Lòn a' Phùinnsein is a stagnant pool, which is always a bad sign. A healthy pool always has an inlet and an outlet, perhaps a stream or even a river running down from the hillside and that same stream or river or manmade channel continuing on the other side towards the sea. But this pool has no outlet, so all the gunge in the world gathers in it, like a cupboard you never clean but fill with rags and rubbish until it festers.

It makes me confront death every day, for otherwise I would avoid it and pretend it doesn't happen, although I know only too well that my calves are born to go to the slaughterhouse and that, sooner or later, even dear Maisie herself, like every other Maisie before her, will end up buried in my trench, or lying on a slab. Which is why I keep calling the lead cow Maisie, because then she lives on forever.

Like my own name. Donald. Dòmhnall. Named after my father, Dòmhnall, who was named after his father Dòmhnall and so on and so on back to the beginning of time, to Dòmhnall MacÀdhamh himself, the son of the father of mankind.

The thing about the poisonous bog is that it declares it's deadly, whereas death itself is more than likely to creep up on you unexpectedly, without warning. So we go around whistling and singing tunes and exercising and all that stuff so as to not to hear him padding about in the background, waiting to pounce. And maybe it's better to be surprised, after all. One knock on the head with a mallet in the byre, and there you go.

Whereas it's more likely to be long and lingering and painful. At least for the cattle and sheep it's quick: nowadays Dr Alick, the vet, soothes them first, but back in the day it was a distraction of hay or fresh corn or some other treat for them while you lined up the hammer blow. Sometimes you can't help but feel pity.

There are so many things the poor cows can die of. Pneumonia, grass staggers, botulism, anaplasmosis, colitis – so many things the vet writes down as the official cause, when often it is just inexplicable. Healthy one day, tired and languid the next, and then passing away. There's always more than we know. And it's down to the trench again to dispose of the carcass. Maisie and I know fine we don't have the best or most productive herd in the world eating the best grass, but it's what we have and we do our best. Maybe we suffer more from knowledge than from ignorance.

When they graze, I sometimes lie on my back and close my eyes, and listen to them munching. It's the most contented sound in the whole universe, and if everyone heard it there would no longer be any wars anywhere, because no one would want to fight or kill anyone while that happy sound goes on.

I teach them, though, to be wary of *Lòn a' Phùinnsein*.

Not to avoid it completely, but to skirt its edge where there is good grass and saplings and heather and thistles. Isn't it odd that the best things are always on the very edge of danger? Where it takes courage. For instance, sometimes I go over east behind the mountains to fish. The best trout and wild salmon are to be found at the very foot of the high crags, which are treacherous to climb. But I've learned how to do it, inch by inch, foot by foot.

We stop at this fourth station, *Lòn a' Phùinnsein*, for as long as we stop at all the others. It reminds me of the beautiful service of the Stations of the Cross we used to have every Sunday evening in my childhood, which has now gone out of fashion like so many other things and only done on special occasions. Here is where Jesus met His Mother. All around the mile I pray and meditate and think. Those fourteen stages are the whole of history, I believe.

We don't extend our stay at *Lòn a' Phùinnsein*. Maisie and the herd sense it. They don't rush off, but their stride becomes that bit longer and without any guidance from me they lead the way over to *Loch na h-Eala* (Swan Loch), where I sail round the world.

6

IT'S THE MOST beautiful loch and banked by the only copse of trees in the place: *Coille a' Challtuinn* (Hazelwood) as it is known. It's a sacred wood, so no one ever cuts down any branch or tree there. A beautiful stone wall keeps livestock and wildlife away. It's where the bees gather in the early summer. They hum softly inside the trees for weeks on end, so that you hear their song long before you see them. You should be here on a May morning. The larks singing and the cuckoos calling from moor to shore and the corn and hay beginning to grow. The day is not long enough for them to sing and grow, so they continue through the clear evening light.

When I was a child I used to come here and swing for hours on end on the branch of the birch tree. Up and down and over and across. I was a pirate and a monkey and a bear and a bird. The tree has grown now and the branch is big and firm but it still sways when I sit on it every day I stop here. I sing a bit as I swing,

'Swing low, sweet chariot, coming for to carry me home.'

They say the old pagans used to worship in this

wood, though that's just bosh. If they worshipped anywhere they would have done so at the next station, where the only pre-historic standing stone in the place is situated. The standing stone hasn't had any wall put round it and has survived cows and sheep scratching themselves against it for centuries. It's worn at the edges where they rub themselves, but the two facing sides (looking east and west) are still faintly decorated with signs and symbols no one can understand any more, if they were ever meant to be understood. There's a hole in the centre of the stone, but no one knows if it was there from the very beginning or hollowed out by time. It hasn't weakened the stone, which stands as solid and permanent as ever.

But the loch is leafy and soft and sheltered, and Maisie and the herd love it. It's their favourite place in the whole world, and if the round mile wasn't so well marked into their memories, I know they'd just head there straightaway every day and spend the whole day there. But I think that would spoil the delight, for it would become common. It's best to come to it in due course.

'*Ann am mionaid, Maisie. Ann am mionaid.*' ('In a minute, Maisie. In a minute.')

The loch is fed by three fresh springs and the stream running from down the mountain, which leaves its water constantly sparkling. On clear days you can see the sky reflected perfectly in the loch, and then look up to see if the loch is also in the sky. It's got a solid shingly edge which gives Maisie and the herd the joy of walking out slowly into it, safe in the knowledge that they won't sink or suddenly vanish into its depths. They edge out bit by bit, lapping up the water and rejoicing in the cleanliness round their hooves and cannon bones and knees. As they wade in the shallows they'll live forever because they're so happy. On a summer's day they remind me of the postcards you see out at the pier shop.

I also drink from the water because it keeps me young. I lie down on my belly and, every day, wonder whether I should lap it up like a dog or cup my hands and drink from it in that more human way. Sometimes I do and sometimes I don't. I resent the way the water trickles through my hands when I drink, as if I'm losing something precious, so mostly I lie down and lap like a dog. Gideon would have sent me home, but Rover approves. Though I keep him well away while I'm lapping.

The loch is full of water-lilies. For most of the year you only see the leaves flat in the water, but come June, July and August they burst into bloom, purple and blue and yellow and white. If I were married, I would pluck a blossom every day and take it home, but instead I go across to the reed bed by the side where the *seileasdairean* (irises) grow, because they make perfect boats.

This is how: you break off an iris leaf and make a slit about an inch long with your nail or a knife along the spine of the thick part of the leaf. Then take the sharp end of the leaf and tuck it into the slit, pull it through, and you have a sail-shape to make a boat. Of course that's just the simplest one, for there are so many different kinds of iris-boats: skiffs with just a leaf-mast, and schooners that have three or four sails, and my favourite, the long Chinese junk made out of three iris leaves bent and tucked and folded one into the other, which sails so well because it's perfectly flat. The boats sail far and strong, dodging the pirates, through the Strait of Malacca. You always need to make a thing stronger than yourself.

I would really need to show you how to do the boats because words are so inadequate. If you saw me doing them a few times I'm sure you could do them yourself, because I know that's the only way to learn. By doing. It's the only way I learned. My mother eventually took my hand and worked me through the turns and loops and slits and slots until it was as natural to me as opening and closing my fist.

But there are so many variations, and each day I try to do a different kind of boat. Instead of looping forwards you can loop it backwards, so that even when you use just one leaf the iris boat looks more like a Chinese junk.

These Chinese boats are beautiful. Simple working things. I saw thousands of them when I was at sea. It was the first thing I did after I left school. Went off and joined the Merchant Navy and spent five years watching the grey waters of the world. O, I know there were days of scorching sun and sparkling waters west and east of Africa, but mostly it was the Atlantic run in all its grey dullness.

What I remember most about arriving on the

mainland for the first time was the big clock at Oban Railway Station. It shone as big as the moon over Easabhal on a winter's night. It was twenty past three in the afternoon, and I stood and watched the big minute hand move round until it struck four o' clock. I then ran and got the 4.15 train to Glasgow.

I liked the East, or the Far East as we called it then, and its glittering seas, which became so dirty and polluted the nearer we came to ports. But what life! Millions of people everywhere on small boats fishing with their little spears and hooks and nets, and if my mother hadn't died and I had to come home to look after Maisie and the herd I would have stayed out there. I especially liked the tea. Ever since, I have gotten a regular supply of Fuchow Golden Needle Black Tea through the post from China.

Every day, when I make a new iris leaf boat and sail it on the loch, I steer it towards one of those faraway places. Yesterday it was to Burma. I sail it down through the North Channel and the Irish Sea and St George's Channel before heading down the west coast of Africa where the currents are so strong. I have to be so careful down by the Canaries Current and the Guinea Current and the Benguela Current which takes me round the Cape, and on then across the great Indian Ocean and the Bay of Bengal. Today I sailed north, to Murmansk, because it was that bit colder, and tomorrow I might go again on that single voyage I made to South America where the kisses and all that stuff attached to them was so hard and brutal.

I'd seen it all since I was a wee boy. The bull was brought in once a year, and at first it was surprising and astonishing to watch. The cows frothing for days on end, wailing and moaning all through the night, until Big Angus arrived first thing in the morning slowly lumbering towards them, and then the sudden mount and that big thing going in and then the quietness after as Angus lumbered across the field to the next bellowing cow and so on and so on through the days.

Maybe that kiss with Mary Ann spoilt it all for me, for ever after I expected that butterfly moment which never happened in any of those places in Cuba or Buenos Aires or Singapore. Just the drink and the attraction, the payment and the disappointment, and the long grey journey back home across the Atlantic.

The one thing I learned at sea was to make my bed as soon as I got up out of it, whether first thing in the morning or at ten minutes to midnight for the night watch, for you never knew when you'd get to bed again – maybe after a long two-day storm – and it was always good then to have a well-made bed with the blanket all ready to fall into. Like the cows having fresh straw for theirs. They like that. My mother had always made my bed for me before I went to sea, and now every morning for the past fifty years I've done it myself, leaving the neighbours surprised at first, and now scoffing at my washing flying in the breeze on the line every single day. If it's not my semmit and long-johns it's one of my towels.

'Fancy that,' I hear them say. 'Home is the sailor, home from the sea.'

Sometimes in the winter when it's all cold outside and warm by the fire I just lie down on the sofa next to it and fall asleep watching the shadow of the flames flickering on the wall and ceiling. I still have the long toast fork grandfather had, and just before I fall asleep I stick a slice of bread on the fork and toast it while lying in bed. I keep the butter in a clay crock at the foot of the bed. I'm older now than he was then, though I'm still a wee boy. As he was too, had I known.

The other thing about the loch is that it's a mirror. On clear days I can see myself as I ought to be seen, shimmering in the water, coming and going. The eyes are mine, but with every movement of the water they're my father's. I don't remember him, because he died six months before I was born, but I know they are his eyes by the way they momentarily appear, then disappear when a sudden wisp of wind strikes the loch. I am young in the water, since the only wrinkles I see are little waves, like voices lapping in the breeze. All the things I heard from Mum and Grandfather move in the water.

'There's always tomorrow,' she said.

And here we are. There are no photographs of them. Not because there were no cameras then, but because they didn't want their photographs taken. I don't need photographs to see them. Grandfather belonged to another time. Another world. I'm the only one who remembers him, his tall lean figure, always carrying a hoe or a spade or a sickle, with his small white beard and the bunnet cocked to one side, against the wind. Turning the soil with a foot plough.

'It works, which is all that matters,' he said.

I cut my hair by the loch. My mum used to cut it and talk about my father as she placed the bowl on my head and shaved round it.

'The best ploughman in the place,' she said.

The other children laughed at me at school after every cut.

'Who ploughed your hair?' they shouted.

'Was it a blind Clydesdale horse?'

Ever since then I've cut my own hair. There's an official hairdresser out at the pier, but she's so nosey. I went there once and it was, 'What's doing this weekend?' and, 'Are you planning to go away this year?' and, 'Did you get a decent price for the stirks at the sale?'

As if it was any of her business. Ever since then I've done it myself.

At first I tried the bowl, but it was impossible. It kept falling off every time I reached round the back. Then one day, as I was sailing to Freemantle across the loch, I didn't put the iris boat knife away back in my pocket. It's a Swiss Army Knife. I bought it all those years ago in Liverpool, after we'd sailed back from Buenos Aires. That was the last time I was on the mainland. It has fifteen parts, which I use at various times for different purposes. Apart from the large and the small blades which I use for slicing things up, I'm constantly using the screwdriver, occasionally the toothpick, whenever a chunk of chop or mutton gets stuck between my teeth, and the scissors to cut odds and ends, including, from that day on the loch, my hair.

I suppose it's part of the reason people look at me and talk about me and call me a fool. Thing is, it's ever so difficult to cut a straight line, a straight rig and furrow like my father, because no matter how hard I try and no matter how still and clear and mirror-like the loch is, my fringe is always skew-whiff when I finish.

'Ach,' I say to myself, 'that bit is still a bit long,' and I cut a bit off that, but then that's too short, and then I do the other side and so on and so on until it looks straight and perfectly rigged and furrowed in the water, but still there it is, a bit up and a bit down when I get home and glance in the mirror. Not that it makes any difference to Maisie anyway, whose own *dosan* hangs over her eyes as the last remaining hippy in the place. The cows' coats grow quicker in the winter to protect them from the wind and cold. Same as my beard, which I grow long every year between Martinmas and Easter.

I was never that good a ploughman anyway. I tried it as soon as I could with a horse and shaft but could never keep the lines as straight as I wanted, and there was always the knowledge that folk kept saying I'd never be as good as my father at it. I wish that could have spurred me on, but it worked the other way with me. I didn't want to sully his memory by becoming as good, if not better than him, because I know how people are. They would then start saying, 'Ach well, the old man hadn't been that good anyway,' and I couldn't bear that hypocrisy, or the burden it would put upon me, like a yoke around my neck. There's no point in being good at something if you don't feel happy about it.

The only other paid employment I've had was as a roadman. I enjoyed that, and even now on our daily walk I try to fix and repair bits as I go along. So many holes and ruts, some washed away in the rain, others eroded by time. You have to repair it in layers. It's no use just sticking in a bit of sod here and there. You have to excavate the fault properly first so that you have hard rock underneath and then fill it up with layers of stones and gravel and grass.

I got the job after coming home from sea. I know fine it was a job that was given to those of us who had no official qualifications and were considered more or less unemployable. Where else would we get jobs, having left school with no O-Levels or anything? We were deemed fit for the pick and shovel, to work on culverts and ditches and what they called roads in those days, which were little better than cart-tracks. They called us the BnB Squad – Brawn and No Brains. You see, that's the difference between a job and a trade. Anyone can do a job, but not everyone has a trade. Otherwise what would be the point of being a herdsman?

A rickety old van driven by the foreman, Jock MacKenzie, picked us all up at the road end at 8.30 every morning and took us to the hut where we spent the first hour or so warming ourselves with mugs of tea and playing darts. Jock had been a policeman in Glasgow and was assumed to have some authority, though he didn't give a damn, seeing he was on a policeman's pension already. He was a wonderful darts player though. He would start off with three treble twenties and his favourite finish was a bullseye and treble seventeen.

I'm not sure we repaired any roads. We'd basically set up one of these roadmen's tents on the verge of the single-track lane. While four of us sat in there playing cards and drinking from our tea flasks, two worked on the road. Or at least looked as if they were working on the road, wearing dark blue overalls and bunnets and digging away, even when it was not needed, with a pick-axe. When some official's car came along one of the men would stand there for ages with his STOP sign while the other hacked away at the road until the driver finally opened the door and complained. The road would then be officially opened for them.

Nevertheless, there was one proper worker there – Archie MacDougall, who had worked with proper road makers on the mainland and knew all about pebbles and stones and quarrying and rocks and explosives and who showed us all how the work was supposed to be done properly. I learned a great deal from him. It's thanks to Archie that the round mile Maisie and the herd and Rover and I navigate every day is in such splendid condition.

7

WE WALK ON another two hundred and twenty-four paces. When I say walk, I don't really mean walk. I mean travel. Maisie and the herd sort of saunter, going sideways and round and about as much as forwards. Although they can run and trot and gallop and jump and swim when they need to.

I like it when they go swimming. I swim them out to Eilean Glas on the other side of the island in early spring when the grass is so much greener there, to give them a good start to the year. I lead, doing the breaststroke, with Maisie following, because she trusts me and then all the herd follow her, because they trust her. They trust the smell of spring in the air. The birds always tell us when spring arrives. They always know it's the right time. Whether it says March or April or May on the calendar makes no difference. Spring arrives when they do, singing their little hearts out. No birds of prey can sing, though. I suppose they're too busy looking for prey to have time for singing.

There are so many ways to travel. I remember my grandfather lifting me up in his two hands and placing me on the big white Clydesdale horse, and whenever I'm up high I still hear his hooves clip-clopping across the yard. I remember my mother's breath on my face as she carried me in the papoose-type sling across her breast. I remember that first little tricycle I had, freewheeling down the hill, tumbling onto the soft grass, and someone laughing as I rolled over and over and over again. Grandfather sowed barley by hand from his *sgùird* (canvas seed bag), like a giant feeding the earth with manna. As he cast the first handful of seed he chanted a prayer. It was strange, because unlike our nighttime prayers, it was not an ask but an answer. '*Dia chuir buil is buaidh is toradh is cinneachdain air*'. ('God (will) make it root and grow and flourish and multiply').

We called Grandfather '*Seanair*'. He spoke like the sea, coming and going from far away in waves. His voice would start slowly and softly and then swell up until it swept onto the sand and then swept back out again. '*O Dhia, Dhòmhnaill, dè idir idir a tha thu ag ionnsachadh san sgoil sin mura bheil fhios agad gu bheil an saoghal cruinn agus nuair a thòisicheas tu rud gu feum thu a thoirt gu ceann cruinn*' 'Good Lord, Donald, what on earth are you learning in that school if you don't know that the world is round and when you begin something you need to bring it to a finish to begin a fresh round.'

The day Miss MacKinnon read *The Arabian Nights* at school, I flew that night on my woollen blanket to Oban. Over Barra and Tiree, passing high above all the MacBrayne's boats down far below in the wild sea and next thing hovering over the railway station where all the trains were puffing away, ready to go to Glasgow and London, and as they puffed out billowing smoke behind them the blanket raced up, leaving the trains far behind. Next thing we were over the Atlantic and I could see towers and palaces and all kinds of bright lights and my best friend Alistair (we all called him Ali), who was with me on the carpet, told me it was New York and asked if I wanted to land there and I said, 'No, can we go on?'

He said, 'Okay then, but it will get much colder the further north we go.' Soon we were over ice and snow and icebergs and frozen houses and villages and cities and lakes and oceans where we saw huge white polar bears and I woke up shivering because the blanket had fallen off the bed and the snow was falling ever so softly on the tiny skylight window above my bed.

You should never walk in a straight line. Folk always think it's the quickest way between any two points, but they're wrong. I learned at sea that the most efficient way between any two points is by doing a great circle. So if you're travelling from Lochboisdale to Valparaiso, for example, you don't just sail in south towards the Sound of Barra and then west across the Atlantic, but you follow the curve of the earth, even if it takes you via Stornoway and Mexico City and Leningrad and all round the world.

And the same here where I walk. For instance, if I'm going to the shop (which is five miles to the north) to get some groceries, I can't just walk out of the house and towards it in a straight line because then I'd have to walk through MacPherson's kitchen, climb over Archie MacDougall's hen house, tunnel through numerous brick walls and outhouses and buildings, whereas instead I turn right and do a great circle round the back of the church, via the side-gate of the Post Office and down by the shoreline to get to my destination.

My grandfather was a wonderful storyteller, and he told me that stories worked the same way. 'You never go from A to B,' he said, 'but from A to Y and then back to B and forward to X and so on and so forth. Because the thing is, Donald, if you look at a dog or a hen or a pig or a cow or a horse or any intelligent human being, they never march forwards in a straight line. They only do that in the army, and do you know why? Because they're marching people to their death. People who are marching into life do the exact opposite, like how a dog sniffs this way and that way along the world. That's where you discover the secrets of life. Where you least expect it. And remember this, Donald: What you believe about a story is always more important than the story itself.'

And he told me this story.

'Once upon a time,' he said, 'there was a young lad called Donald who lived with his family and all his friends on a small rocky island in the North Atlantic. At the top of the island on the highest rock there was a castle. And in that castle lived the ogre. He was called *Am Fuamhaire*, which means The Giant.

'The *Fuamhaire* and all his friends used to go off on their ships across the waters where they killed everyone they met and brought all their treasures back with them. The castle, they said, was loaded with gold and silver and coins and crowns and diadems and all kinds of wonderful things. And it was locked and guarded by a thousand fierce warriors who all carried swords and shields and spears.

'"Why should we be sitting here starving when he is up there with all the food and money in the world?" Donald's father said. And everyone agreed with him. So, they made a plan to attack the castle and kill the *Fuamhaire* and get the food and treasures for themselves.

'But it seemed impossible, no matter how they tried. They made ropes and tried to climb up the ramparts, but the ropes were never long enough. They tried tunnelling their way in using spades and picks and explosives, but the further they got, the harder the rock became. They made parachutes and planes and flew over and tried to drop in from above, but the whole castle was covered with impenetrable glass made of fire that burnt up any human or implement that landed on it.

'Eventually, they were at the point of starvation. Then Donald woke up one night and said to himself, "You know the one thing we haven't tried is the front door." So, first thing in the morning, even before he had his gruel for breakfast, he got out of bed and walked up to the castle, which was all quiet and silent, save for owls hooting and bats flying about. He was scared stiff but still he walked on, expecting any moment to be stopped and killed by a horseman or a spear or a rock or a bullet. But all was silent.

'And he walked up to the big doors and tried the handle, which opened as soon as he touched it, and he walked in to find the whole place empty except for tables laden with bread and fruit and wine and sweets and every goblet made of gold and every chair made of silver. Going up to the highest point of the castle, he stood and told the whole world that there never had been a *Fuamhaire*, and if they'd tried the front door years ago, all this would have been theirs.'

Later on, I wondered if he'd been talking about Catrìona and Eòghainn and Mary Ann and me and how happy everything could be if we only believed it. If we'd only walked through the front door, the castle would have been filled with the sound of feasting, pigs and chestnuts roasting on the fire, a piper on the ramparts and children playing hula-hoop and cartwheels in the yard.

This place we stop at after the loch is called *Cnoc nan Òran*. The Hillock of Song. It's where the heather is most abundant and where the birds gather. Isn't it wonderful that despite the almost complete absence of trees, almost every bird in the universe can be found here? Teals and mallards and grouse and corncrakes and shearwater and shags and grebes and kites and sparrowhawks and plovers and sanderlings and dunlins and terns and cuckoos and owls and thrushes and robins and pipits and O, the list goes on and on. Birds you only normally see on the shore sing here as well as the ones of the moor. It's as if their usual natural environment is irrelevant because all the other birds of the air, distant cousins and strangers, are here, singing their hearts out.

Sand and shore and heather and moss and stone and bog and loch and stream and river and sea and air are all one to them, and as they sing above me they tell me that I'm fine here too in this tiny corner of the universe, which is the whole world to me. When they sing from on high, good weather is on the way. When low, wet weather. Sometimes they're silent, knowing when to sing and when not to sing. That doesn't mean anything weather-wise. It's just that they're too busy foraging or feeding their young, or maybe fed up or tired. Some folk think I believe the birds and the clouds tell me what to do. They don't. They just tell me when it's best to do some things, like fixing the gate or the gable end chimney, because of a coming wind.

The mistake people make now is to call the weather 'It'. I don't know if it comes from English television or what, but folk around here now all say 'It's going to rain' or 'It's going to be a nice dry day tomorrow' or wet or windy or whatever the TV man had said. But the thing is, they've forgotten that in Gaelic the weather is a woman. *'The i a' dol a bhith brèagha a-màireach.'* ('She's going to be beautiful tomorrow.') In fact, when I think about everything, nothing is an 'It'. The moon is a woman. And the sun. The land is a man. As is the sea.

'Makes it all human, *nach eil sin ceart* (isn't that right), Rover? Just like you and me.'

And he wags his tail and coories in that bit nearer to me.

Weather is relevant to me in relation to what it does

to the land. When I look out the window first thing in the morning I ask, '*A-nist, a Dhomhnaill, dè tha an t-side ag ràdh riut an-diugh?*' ('Now, Donald – what's the weather saying to you today?'). Sun is good for drying the peats and helping the crops grow, but too much burns everything up and the grass becomes yellow and withered. Same with wind and rain. You want small rain. Enough to cool the herd and irrigate the land, but too much drowns the earth. It's best when the thin rain plays tig, coming in sometimes from the west, sometimes from the east, having fun. Feeding showers. Showers that feed the earth. I remember the bright summer days best.

It's no wonder the young people hold their annual music festival here. In the old days it was the site of the horse and cattle fair, with drovers from all over travelling here to buy and sell, accompanied (as is the music festival now) by all kinds of tramps and hawkers with their booths, selling cups and saucers and clocks and shawls and potions.

For us children there was a man in a multi-coloured tent selling balloons. He sat outside the tent in a large wicker basket attached to a balloon and claimed that he'd flown in that way and would depart the same way during the night when we were all asleep. For sixpence, he allowed us to climb into the basket and then pulled at some strings and ropes for a while, shouting 'Whoohoo' and 'Wheee – here we go, right up into the clouds; if we touch the sun shout out, "Loud!"' And we'd all shout out 'Loud!' once we got near the sun, as he stashed our sixpences away in his pouch. He had a parrot called Blind Pew on his left shoulder crying out 'Pieces-of-Eight, Pieces-of-Eight' all day long.

After that, a travelling circus came round for a while and stopped here. We young men went just to see the scantily clad lady acrobat who did somersaults across the floor, then pirouetted on a thin rope tied across the top of the tent. She was beautiful and could stand on her toes as she danced across the rope, and we all tried it afterwards on a fishing rope laid out on the ground and none of us could do it. One year the tent blew down in a gale and the circus never returned.

The new music festival is for young people, so I don't go. Not that I'm forbidden or anything, just that I can hear the music from my house during the weekend it's on, and it's too loud for me. No, not just that. It belongs to young people, as the fair belonged to my grandfather, and the circus to me and my school friends. It was our space, where we were allowed to be young. Just as the round mile is the space where I am allowed to be old.

I like space. I wear loose clothing to give my body space to breathe. I prefer braces to a belt because they don't tighten my belly. Once a month I light a fire outside and burn everything I haven't used for seven days, so that there is always plenty of space in the house. I try to make space itself the thing rather than put things into it. It's what happens up in the sky too. I watch the clouds all gathering together, pushing each other closer and closer until there is no room for them to move. When that happens, they burst and pour out all that water so that the skies are empty again. Compare that to the nice bright summer days when the clouds give space to each other to breathe and exist and look beautiful as they float like soft bog-cotton in the sky. I've watched the clouds for fifty years and never seen one exactly like the other. Oh, they might look the same at a glance, but when you really look, they never are. I don't suppose any of us are either, forever shifting around. I like it when it's wet and windy and dull and dreich, and no one is to be seen because they're all inside watching television or reading or whatever they do, and there's only me and Maisie and Rover and the herd outside to feel all the elements as they pour and swing at us with all their might.

I'm lucky though, because I've got big feet and most folk keep well clear of me in case I stand on them, like the ogre in the story. I wonder if the desire for proper space is what's driving the building of the spaceport. The world has become too crowded, except for here. But if I believe what I read, outer space is already filled with all our rubbish. If I ever get the chance to go up there in a rocket I'll have a bonfire as in my back garden to get rid of it all.

What does a man need but a roof over his head and a fire and a bed and a chair and a table? And when it comes to the kitchen, a pan and a mug and a spoon and a knife. And a change of clothing. All the rest is luxury. Although I accumulate like everyone else. I must have hundreds of knives, forks and spoons, including the untouched silver set my mum got from her aunt on the day of her wedding, and drawers full of socks and pants and ties and jerseys, and loads of ornaments my mum had, which I dust and clean every Saturday night, especially the two china dogs that sit on the ends of the mantlepiece and which were her pride and joy. My walls are covered in pictures and drawings I do with charcoal or pencil of all the cows and dogs and walking-sticks I've had over the years, and I like looking at them and remembering and smiling at all their individual ways when the long winter evenings come. I walk 'round the room in the glow of the fire, which makes it look as if they are all walking about in the sunset or in the early blue light of dawn, depending if the fire is just newly lit and rising up or already well-lit and settled nice and quiet with a steady reddish glow. The thing about sunrise and sunset is that you have a bit of night and a bit of day at the same time until one gives way to the other.

'After you,' one says.
'No. No, after you.'
'Okay, then. I'm off to sleep now.'
'See you later, then.'
'Okay. See you soon. Bye.'
'Bye.'

8

THERE'S ANOTHER REASON why I walk this round mile every day. It has to do with a story my mother told me, and every day Catrìona and Eòghainn and I are baffled that we can't change the story. This is the story as my mum told me.

A boy went to see this girl, who was standing inside her house with the window open.

'Will you go out with me?' he asked her, and the girl replied,

'When I've lifted the linen, lowered the glass and put the dead to bury the living, then I will.'

And the boy, dismayed, gave up hope and left and sailed to foreign parts.

Returning, after a voyage of three years, he heard she was married to another, but unhappily. So, he went to see her and asked why she hadn't agreed to go out with him.

'All I said,' she said, 'was that I would be with you as soon as I cleared the linen off the table and shut the window and smoored the fire, and that would have only taken minutes. But you didn't understand, and left.'

The ruins of the house where the girl lived are on the way, lying between the hillock of songs and the shore. She's called Catrìona and stands forever in that open window looking out towards the horizon. She has auburn hair and light green eyes that light up every time she sees me coming, but lose their light when she sees I'm not Eòghainn. There's no anger, just regret. There's unfinished business. That without happiness the world will perish.

"*'S tu fhèin a th' ann*' ('It's yourself'), she says, and I say,

"*'S e.*' ('It is.')

'*Agus ciamar a tha thu an-diugh?*' ('And how are you today?') she asks.

'Like the wind,' I say. 'Coming and going.'

'He never comes,' she says. 'I must have frightened him away.'

'No. He was just stupid. Daft and impatient.'

She laughs.

'I have all the patience in the world. All the time in the world.'

And I sit there, silent, for ages and ages.

'Why...?' I begin to ask, 'did you speak in riddles?'

'Riddles?'

'You could have put it plainly: when I've set the table, closed the window and smoored the fire.'

She looks at me with disdain. The way Maisie looks at me when I do something foolish.

'What? And forsake song and poetry and language and romance and all that is good and fine in the world?'

'Which you lost.'

'No. I still have it. Hope is always on the horizon.'

'Which turns out to be me. Poor old me.'

'I too was impatient then. So now I wait for him with everlasting patience.'

'Until?'

'For a year and a day. Until the story changes. As long as I believe he'll come back, he will.'

And then she vanishes, and I go into the ruins of the house where the table is beautifully laid with a steaming bowl of porridge in the middle and Eòghainn sitting there pouring fresh creamy milk onto it while Catrìona arranges some flowers in a vase and the fire burning away with the smell of peat and the glass window all open with a warm breeze moving the lace curtains, beyond which we can all hear the birds singing pill-iù-pill-ill-ill-ill.

'The song of the redshank,' Catrìona says, and sings,

'Pill iù Pill ill ill ill Eòghainn
Pill iù Pill ill ill ill Eòghainn
Pill iù Pill ill ill ill Eòghainn
Pill ill èadhainn pill ill ill o h-eòin
Pill iù Pill ill ill ill Eòghainn
Pill iù Pill ill ill ill Eòghainn
Pill iù Pill ill ill ill Eòghainn
Pill ill èadhainn pill ill ill o h-eòin...'

And on and on until I go over the brae which makes the house invisible, and all is silent once again.

9

OVER THE BRAE is the shoreline, where Maisie and the herd eat seaweed. Catrìona's song is interrupted by the sound of the waves crashing endlessly onto the sand and the thin cries of the numerous shore birds – oystercatchers and sanderlings and dunlins and turnstones and seagulls. The gulls constantly carry shellfish inland in their beaks and then let them drop and smash on the rocks so they can eat what's inside – mussels and cockles and clams and crabs. The broken shells lie there as evidence that shore and sea are the same. It's odd. Each thing is itself yet part of something bigger.

From here the sea looks grey. Yet when I go out in my boat it's blue and green and silver and azure and all kinds of colours. If you didn't know fish lived in it, you'd never guess by looking from a distance.

The coastline has eroded forty yards since I was a child. The grass on the shore's edge is rich and full of nutrients and causes Maisie and the herd to belch and fart all day long when they eat it. I see on television that they are to blame for global warming and climate change, though I doubt my seven poor cows have much to do with it. Out at sea an oil tanker sails south from

Shetland. When I was at sea we used to play cards when we were off watch. Cribbage was my favourite. You can play it on your own too and sometimes beat yourself.

Despite all the noise and tumult, the world feels empty. Houses that used to be filled with families are uninhabited or serve as holiday homes for weekend visitors. It reminds me of that story where it was always day at one end of the village and night at the other. Fields stand unploughed and untilled. I'm alone here, as I'm alone in the house and on my round mile walk despite Maisie and the herd, and Rover and Wilhelmina and Seasaidh Bhaile Raghnaill and Dòmhnall and my grandfather with his big white Clydesdale horse and Mary Ann and *Mac Talla nan Creag* and Catrìona and Eòghainn and all the birds of the air and the moor and the seals and dolphins that cry and splash around me in the water and the jets that leave their fading white trails above me in the sky. The clouds are so far away. There's a great absence. So many things never get a chance to be said.

That's how it is. Nor does it make my friends imaginary. They are as real to me as these old boots I wear and as the stick I hold in my hand as I sit here by the shore and as the phut-phut-phut of that lobster-boat engine I hear and see out there hauling in the creels just now. That's Johnnie, who lives in Ardmore and supplies the local hotel with prawns and lobsters every day. 'There's fish in the sea for everyone,' is all he says any time I see him. Sometimes he drops a bag of mackerel off for me at the end of my road and I eat them with potatoes.

There is no such thing as a meal without potatoes. Though they have to be the right kind. Dry, floury ones. I can't stand these wet ones, which are tasteless. The best are the machair-grown potatoes, hand-drilled in late spring after you've fertilized the ground with seaweed. Horse manure is best, though it's hard to get here nowadays. They grow beautifully in the sandy soil. I don't think any other ground in the whole world is more suited to them. Not even Ireland. Thank God for Sir Walter Raleigh I say every time I harvest a basinful of them. Once folk stop planting potatoes and keeping cows it will be a poorer world.

I watch television. Usually with the sound off, because I'm busy with something else. Darning my socks or washing my underwear or preparing dinner. And they too look all alone out there, speaking silently into cameras while thousands of people like me go about their own business, carving chickens, playing cards or talking to their dogs. Nothing is trivial. Anyway, the news they have isn't the news at all. It's just the news from there, not from here. TV is more of a mystery to me than the fairy knoll. Though maybe it's the same thing, except from far away. And if it was the news from here, who would tell it anyway? Probably Uilleam MacIsaac who thinks he knows what's important, when he doesn't know the first thing about cows, for instance. I think those who speak a lot do so because they only have the one thing to say, over and over again. Anyone who's unsure what anything means keeps just keeps quiet. Janet Smith, for example. She doesn't say much, except to the hens, who always agree with her.

Sometimes I have the television sound on, and it proves they're just doing the same as me. Telling stories. All about plans and proposals and strategies for starting this war here, or stopping that one over there. What they say is too small to account for anything. What do I know anyway about Israel or Syria or any of these places? There must be herdsmen like me wandering about with their cows in the hills and mountains over there wondering what's happening. I never see them on the screen, just those politicians explaining it all and doctor after doctor holding a wounded child and crying. When I get bothered by something on TV I look out the window and watch Miss Smith feeding the hens. They trust her. Rely on her.

It's wrong to say the television people live in a different world, because they don't. They eat and walk and cry and dream and hope and imagine just like I do, with their own Janet Smiths to contend with, their own round mile to walk and navigate each day where they make peace with their own Mary Anns and Catrìonas.

And it's not a matter of distance or geography or language either, for I also watch television and listen to the radio in Gaelic, and all that also seems strange and alien and far away to me. I recognize the words but can't make sense of them, because the words they use could also mean the opposite of what they're saying, and I've no doubt that if they were to join Maisie and Rover and me on my daily round I would make little sense to them either. This is my whole world, as theirs is theirs.

Gloic. Amadan. In fact, Nurse MacLeish called in to see me a while back, making up some excuse about an NHS form, though she and I knew fine she was checking my mental health.

'How are you, Donald?'

'Oh, fine, fine.'

And I made her a cup of tea and took the box of Digestive Biscuits down from the shelf and told myself not to dip them into my cup, though she did. I suppose that was to try to put me at ease, though it just put me on edge. What did she know? What did I do wrong? And it's not as if we were friends or anything, when you could do that kind of thing. With relative strangers you behaved properly and just didn't pick your nose or scratch yourself all over the place, so Mum told me.

'You walk a lot?' she said.

'Aye. The cows need grass and air and exercise.'

'And yourself?'

'Me too. Except for the grass. I don't eat that. But mostly I stop and stand and watch the cows. The seven cows.'

She sipped her tea.

'We're always walking somewhere,' I added. 'Not just wandering about.'

'Do you see many folk during the day, Donald?'

I always get suspicious when folk use my name in a sentence. She might certify me and send me away to that institution on the mainland from which very few ever return. Or if they do they come back changed. Quiet and subdued.

'Not really. Just depends who's around.'

She looked at me, but didn't say anything.

'Well then,' she said, after a while, 'if you just fill in that form at your leisure you can take it along to the surgery when you can. Or I'll call in for it next time I'm passing. Probably on Friday.'

You should never say too much. Only what's necessary. I said that once to Nurse MacLeish.

'So how do you decide?' she asked.

My father had three cousins who were shepherds and lived in an even more remote village over the hill. It's abandoned now. They were men of few words. If you met Angus and said,

'Hello,'

all you'd get was,

'Uhh.'

And when you met George and said,

'Nice day, eh?'

he'd grunt,

'Uhh.'

And the youngest brother, Murdo, was at school with me and at first I used to say to him,

'Fancy playing football, Murdo?'

'Uhh.'

And off he'd march up and over the hill.

When they were cleared from the land by MacIver the Factor they headed off to Australia on an emigrant ship, which seems to have been full of the riff-raff of the world and sailed through some of the wildest storms recorded in history. It was a drunken crew and Angus,

George and Murdo were forced to speak properly or be thrown overboard like Jonah. The skipper had a plank of wood which he sometimes nailed to the poop, threatening passengers with a traditional sea death. The crew mutinied, and they were such bad sailors that my cousins pleaded on their knees in their own fluent divine speech to be set free from the noisy ship, and they were released down the side with an emergency raft. Eventually they were washed ashore on an empty forested island, which suited them perfectly. So they set to work, each silently on his own, thinking about all the chaos and words forced on them on their long voyage. Despite everything, it had been exciting, building their own little homesteads and tilling and harvesting the soil and the sea. After seven years Murdo looked up and said,

'I can hear a cow lowing.'

George and Angus just looked at him and were tempted to say 'Uhh,' but said nothing and went back to work. So seven years later George said,

'Where?'

And again they were silent.

Seven years on, Angus said,

'Look here – if you guys don't quieten down everyone in the world will hear us and throw us out of here.'

'Uhh. Uhh,' the other two said.

I sometimes walk out to the ruins of their old cottage and cry with them.

I watched Nurse MacLeish drive away in her red car until it disappeared over the hill. Strange how you see a thing for a while and then it goes out of sight, though you can still see it as it was, the silver bumper glinting in the sun as it climbed the brae and then slowly vanished into the mist. Sometimes it happens more slowly. One day you see a caterpillar crawl across the grass, the next a pale blue butterfly is flying through the air.

The shoreline is the opposite of that. It's as if I can see forever when I'm there: north to Darkland, south to Lightland, west as far as Rockall, and east, beyond the hills, are Russia and Siberia. I sailed there once, to Archangel, though they say it with a 'k' sound, which we don't have in Gaelic, where we loaded with timber to take back to Leith. A Soviet woman counted the logs as they came on board, as did our First Mate. Though she counted twice as many, so we had to pay for double what we bought. We didn't argue.

I suppose you can make figures up anyway, just like everything else. I sometimes pass the time doing the times table. Two times two makes four all the way up to twelve times twelve makes one hundred and forty four, though then I vary it and miss the times out and just recite two-twos-four all the way to twelve-twelves-one hundred and forty-four. We never learned past the twelve times table in school, so when it comes to thirteen I have to do with a pencil and paper, which I can only do at home because I don't carry them with me on my round.

The Archangel Michael looks after me. He is my patron saint, and I always know his touch when I sign my full name, Donald Michael MacDonald. He watched over me as I signed the NHS form for Nurse

MacLeish, blessing me with the special powers he has – courage and strength. I lack these so much. When I write the letter M in our name I do it big to honour him. He will be able to pray better than me. Probably in Latin and English and Chinese and in every other language too. Though God will understand my simple Gaelic prayers just as well as his big anointed ones.

Here on the shoreline, the strand runs for miles and miles, and in the olden days we used to have horse races. I remember them from childhood. Men, women, children and hundreds and hundreds of ponies out for the *Oda* – the annual horse races – at Michaelmas.

That's the end of September, and no wonder the people celebrated then, for the harvest was in, and only a long bleak winter ahead. These days it's a perpetual harvest, for when I take an occasional trip out to the big shop it's full of autumn fruits all year round. And I can never get over the colours – the vegetable boxes full of red and green and yellow things I never used to see growing down on our machair, where the potatoes were either brown or white, the carrots red or white, and everything else green.

Hardly anyone grows anything anymore, and why would they when they can buy them easily in the shop without having to tire themselves growing them? The machair stretches out before me as a tourist spot rather than a workplace. For a moment, I see Mac Iain Chaluim and his seven children working the field, himself on the scythe and his wife and daughters binding and the lads making the sheaves and stacks, but it was only a cloud of dust brought in by the wind. A corncrake calls. It's not the loss that grieves me but the beauty of it all.

Everyone gets home deliveries now. It's all that's left of human contact. A weekly visit from the van driver or the postie, if we're lucky. The rest is television. We used to remember things together. Now TV remembers it for us.

Maybe Nurse MacLeish is right. What if I'm only seeing the dead now, and not the living. As if there's any difference, for look, on one side of me here is the sea and on the other side the moor, and they're the same world. One moves constantly and the other sits still, though I know enough to know that the heather and rocks on the moor are all moving invisibly like everything else in the universe. When Maisie and the herd lie down and I sit watching them it only appears as if we're still. They're chewing the cud and eternally twitching and scratching themselves, and I'm sometimes thinking, sometimes away with the fairies. There's no better sight in the world than to see the full moon shining on the sea. Something greater than ourselves.

I have good eyesight and can see far. One, two ... no, when I really look and my eyes get accustomed to the horizon there are a dozen ships out there, half of them ploughing north, half south. Three oil tankers and three container ships going south. The ferry, four fish-farm vessels and a cruise liner heading north. By the way, Grandfather worked five cardinal points: north, east, south, west and centre. Centre always being the place where he stood.

And then, over on the other side, on the moor, the

stags and hinds high up on the hill and the ruins of all those cottages from centuries ago. Ruins everywhere. What was that word Nurse MacLeish used again, as if in the passing? Dislocated – that was it. She was examining my thumb, that time I hit it with the hammer, but I felt she was talking about me.

'We'd better put a splint on it to prevent further damage. It will fix its way back naturally by the end of the week.'

They were different people, those who lived by the shore and those who lived on the hill. The shore people wary, cautious – exposed to so many gales and winds, looking forever out to sea hoping their fathers, husbands, sons, brothers would return, and those living up there on the hill, secure beneath the shelter of the crags, the deer sniffing the air in the misty mornings, their sheep and cattle eternally grazing through the growing heather.

And then, all of a sudden, roads were built and you could move from one to the other in a jiffy, roaring down the hillside on a quad bike or in a 4x4 and travelling up the other way in a jeep or tractor. You didn't need to be anywhere anymore because you could be everywhere. And maybe I got lost in that transfer, remaining fixed where I am, neither here nor there. Neither a mountain man nor a seaman, but a man of the plains, these flatlands that go on and on and on. It's probably why I like the old cowboy pictures, of wild frontiers that stretch beyond the horizon, where no laws apply and you just get rid of whatever stands in your way. We're almost in America anyway, over the sea there. I even ordered a cowboy hat through the post, and wear it when out herding my own ranch.

The difficulty I have with cowboy films is that things are always being destroyed in them. Either one side is rustling cattle or the other side is killing the rustlers. Or the cowboys are killing all the Indians, or the Indians are killing all the cowboys, and then they take revenge. Or there are fights to the death at places like the OK Corral. Nothing is ever being built up, and where corn or wheat or homesteads are built it's always at the expense of some native or incomer who needs to be cleared. But the cattle always look wonderful, roaming there in their thousands and thousands.

I can tell at a glance if Maisie and the herd are well. They have that sheen about them then, even in the pouring rain. Especially in the scudding rain which washes everything clean, when their coats glisten and their hooves squelch in the mud, and they shake their heads and tails in that fun way of theirs, flinging off the drops of water the way they do with flies in the summer heat. And then when any of them is sick I notice it immediately by the way the head hangs down a bit and the droop of the tail and the slowness of their movement. A glance at the colour and texture of their dung tells me how well they are. Their illnesses are often mild and cured by a tub of water with ten spoons of sugar and a teaspoon of salt. I'm convinced they sometimes feign illness to get that treat.

'You pussycat,' I say to Maisie then, and she looks at me with disdain.

I don't know how Nurse MacLeish thought I was unwell. I'm physically fine, so people must have talked. Gossiped. Which is addictive, like tobacco. They must have had reason. Otherwise, Nurse MacLeish wouldn't be here.

'He's on his own, you know.'

'Just him and those cows.'

'Talks to them.'

'That's natural enough, isn't it?'

'Aye, but. There's talk and talk …'

'Have you heard him then?'

'No. But – it's not just a word here and there. A constant stream. I can hear it from over the hill.'

'They don't talk back, do they?'

And the small chuckles and the almost invisible shake of the head and the glances away, as if they've suddenly noticed something else on the horizon when I come into view. I like Nurse MacLeish, despite my anxiety with strangers. Knew her when she was younger – the daughter of Elsie Campbell who was the district nurse herself here years and years ago. Elsie was big pals with my mother. Patricia went away to Glasgow and married a fellow, MacLeish, who was killed in an accident at the shipyard, and she came back to work here after that. So she knows me, or at least knows who I am. Where you spend your childhood makes you local. Gives you a past. The world isn't that big anyway. It reaches from the top of Easabhal up there out to the sea's horizon on the west. Something like ten miles on a clear day.

I'm not sure how to put this, but I think she cares

for me in the same way I care for Maisie and the herd. They're my patch, my world, and of course I notice when things are well or ill. There's no finer sight in the whole world than to be down on the machair on a fine spring morning watching Maisie and the herd feast on the growing clover. All is fine and well with the world and it's going to last forever and ever, these small white clouds on the horizon hanging like washing in the heavens and the wind soft and warm and the sea all blue and glassy and me sitting there whittling a stick with my Swiss Army Knife and whistling my favourite tune, Father John MacMillan of Barra, into the air.

It may have to do with horizons and boundaries and limits. My croft, on the north side, ends at the stream. On the other side, Norman's croft begins. On the south side I have a stone wall, on the other side of which is the common machair. My croftland runs to the main road on the east side and to the south the boundary is fenced. So the territory is clear and defined. I walk Maisie and the herd on the common grazing which straddles the shore and the hill: land which belongs to us all, but which I use most of all. Things need to have edges. Otherwise I wouldn't know where one thing ends and another starts. I wouldn't know whether to sleep on the bed or on the floor, or whether to eat the loaf of bread or the knife I cut it with. I might not even know the difference then between Maisie and Rover.

On the first day of May I take Maisie and the herd down to the machair to feast on the orchid and poppy-filled sweet grass for ten days and then take them to the high moor to feast on the heather. We treat these days as holidays. As Holy Days which sustain us for the rest of the year. Maisie and the herd are only as good as the feed they get. The grass they graze on is the best there is here and its goodness sustains them for a while. Same with me. After some time at *Lòn a' Phuinnsein* I'm wary for a while that everything is soiled. And after some time at *Cnoc nan Òran* I sing to myself for a while and after being at the Fairy Knoll everything glows with light and sound and softness and hope.

I'm the only one who resisted the new wind farm development. Everyone else took the money, though I refused to budge. Not that it made any difference. It's a company called Clean Green Energy Solutions, and they even offered to name one of the pylons after me, as well as the money. To save them the bother of going to compulsory purchase once everyone else agreed.

'We'll officially christen it "Donald's Dream", in Gaelic if you want, or "The Cowman's Power", or something like that?"

'*Stob Dhòmhnaill*?' I suggested.

I didn't want their money or blessing, but I have got their pylons. Even the poor birds keep clear of them.-

It would be wrong for me to encroach on my neighbours' land. It would be like going into their home and settling myself down on their sofa with my dirty feet up on their stove, or like wandering in and lying on their bed. It would be ignorant and unseemly. So, of course, none of us do that. But then again if we weren't able to do things that were wrong I don't suppose we'd have anything to think or say or do, because everything would then be perfect and not needing any of us at all.

Maybe it's the same with our ways. You see the living, not the dead. You talk to those who are visible, not invisible. Not that there is much difference anyway. Sometimes it's a curse to see everything. Sometimes a blessing. You hear and see what others hear and see, as well as what you alone can see. You believe or disbelieve what you see or hear. Except, when I think about it, what others hear and see is a mystery to me. And you can't touch the mysteries. You can only glimpse them now and again up on the altar when the priest raises them out of the tabernacle to share them with us for a sacred moment. I used to peep up and look through my fingers when I was a child, but now I stay bowed all the way through. I'm glad there's still a place where mystery is at the heart of the matter. Like when we all sing a hymn together I no longer hear or see myself or Miss Smith or anyone else I know, but we somehow become one, just like the communion wafer. Maybe the fairy knoll is like that – a mystery that can only be seen by believers? Who can tell what Nurse MacLeish (or for that matter anyone) hears when she listens to me, or sees when she looks at me? How am I to know what's significant or not?

If she's anything like me, she'll hear one thing and think another and see one thing and always connect it with something else. It's not that association game we played when we were wee so that when Allan said 'cow' I would say 'bull' and when Iain said 'sheep' I said 'dung'.

It's more as if two completely different things come to me simultaneously, so that if I watch a sunset, for example, I think of the pink rouge my mother used to dab on her cheeks any time she went out to something like church where she needed to dress up, or if I hear the sound of a motorbike in the distance I hear my grandfather shaving himself, the open razor grazing the stubble on his cheek with a rasp. He always left his moustache, which he turned up at the ends into an S shape with candle wax. I remember things because I have nowhere else to put them.

I suppose it's memory and desire getting sort of mixed up, as if the things that happened once upon a time could happen again – do happen again, and again – so that time is like the stream behind the house which dries up all summer but then runs over as soon as the first rains of winter arrive, saturating everything around it. Things take time to open and close. Take summer, for example. I always smell the end of summer before I see it. It's usually around the end of August, though sometimes it stretches well into September and, all of a sudden as it were (though it's not), there's a hint of frost in the air and I begin to think of lighting the fire again, though I know it's only an early wave from autumn. She'll take a few weeks yet before she knocks properly on the door. It's usually three fortnights, when summer begins to lock its things away and autumn begins to unlock her doors and windows and byres. We used to call it the carrying south of the year, but I never hear that from anyone nowadays. Sometimes in September through October we get a warm spell when we all feel young again, the cows becoming calves and the sheep lambs in the soft evening light.

So when mum's voice in the kitchen calls upstairs, 'Donald. It's time,' it's not something I imagine, but hear, like I hear the church bells ringing on Sunday morning. And after I climb out of bed and wash and dress and go down the stairs, that mint perfume I smell is as real as the warm smell of manure that meets me when I go out to the byre to see Maisie and the herd. Every Sunday after Mass I come home believing that everything I think and do has eternal consequences. That things matter. Church is the only place where we do something together using the same language and rituals. There used to be the peat-cutting and hay-gathering and sheep-shearing, but machines do all that now. I suppose the pub does that too, though I never go there these days. The third glass is the one that kills.

Not instantly of course. One thing doesn't necessarily lead to another immediately. It might take weeks or years or centuries to happen. Like when you sow potatoes it takes months before you can eat them. Or if you bless or curse someone, maybe it's their great-great-great grandchildren who will feel the consequences. I'm blessed, for example, because my great-great-grandfather, when he was on the verge of emigrating with hundreds of others to Canada, was given this croft by a childless neighbour of his. If that hadn't happened I wouldn't be here walking Maisie and the herd round the mile every day with Rover. If I existed at all I suppose I'd be a farmer on the Canadian Prairies sitting all day in one of those big combine harvesters.

I liked last Sunday's homily. The priest preached on my favourite saying of Jesus – 'What shall it profit a man if he gains the whole world, and loses his own soul.' And Father John said the soul wasn't some sort of airy-fairy thing hanging about in the air, but was as real as the pews we were sitting on and the hands and feet and heads and breath of our fellow worshippers and was measured by how we treated each other as well as our sheep and cows and dogs and crops and that the way not to lose it is to look after and care for and love all these things as best we can. We sang that great hymn, 'Praise my Soul, the King of Heaven', and the birds of the air outside sang with us because they too were happy, and the sun was shining. I'm sure I could hear Maisie and the herd lowing and Rover barking and Wilhelmina purring as we all sang.

Oh, I know fine there's a thin line between things: only a tiny stream separates my croftland from Norman's, and one step takes me across, but when I take that step I become more cautious, walking on someone else's land. I think the danger is when you lose that distinction and one place becomes like the other, and everything becomes yours to possess and not to admire. It has to have a life of its own, which you can desire, but not claim. And if that's the way it is, it often opens the gate and welcomes you in.

'Come in, Donald. It's so good to see you. Take a seat and enjoy. And how are things anyway?'

Things are fine, I told Nurse MacLeish.

'People are saying things,' she said.

'Pah! People!'

'Still,' she says. 'People talk, and rumours get round. They're concerned.'

'Concerned? They should mind their own business.'

'Maybe it is their business, Donald. Our business.'

'Doesn't harm them, does it?'

'Hmmm. You never know what harms people.'

'My thoughts? My ways? Their own?'

She didn't say anything.

'They don't have to think about them or hear them or believe them,' I said.

'No,' she said. 'But maybe they think you're part of them and they are part of you and therefore involved in the same... stories?'

I laughed.

'And you?'

'I'm just concerned, Donald. That it doesn't spill over into the fantastic. The delusional, to use the nursing phrase. You know the way a stream or a river sometimes overflows and floods the fields, making them useless.'

I wanted to say it's good to water the land, but I didn't. I suppose she was concerned about me the same way I'm concerned about my cows. That my knowledge and expertise and experience – for looking after cattle is what I know, it's my trade and profession, if you want to call it that – is not shamed or brought into disrepute. Which it would be if one of my animals were unwell and I just ignored it or was sick and I left it to fend for itself. And the same applies to my neighbour's cows and sheep – if I ever see one acting strangely or in danger or distress, of course I help.

Maybe she's right after all and we do belong to one another. Though it's more likely we're like Lilliput and Brobdingnag which I remember reading about in school, where small people and big people inhabit different islands and poor old Gulliver has to be big where they're wee and wee where they're big, leaving everyone at sixes and sevens. Surely it can't be that only small people should live on small islands and big people on big islands with no exchange between them? Everything doesn't need to be ordinary or average.

I'm a tall man, though I'm not conscious of it until a passing child asks me to lift down a football which has become stuck on the roof of the shed or reach down into the depths of the loch to rescue the toy boat they were playing with.

'Thanks, Mister,' they say, taking the length of my arms for granted.

'I think the best way to look at it, Donald,' Nurse MacLeish said, 'is to remember your stream and stone wall and road and fence, and to know that these are two separate areas of land.'

'Like my head and feet?' I said.

She laughed.

'Like that gate out there,' she said. 'You can close it or open it, depending whether you're coming or going. If you want to keep things in or let them out. Just don't get stuck on either side, eh, Donald Michael?'

I liked the way she included my archangel's name. It

was like a blessing from her. She wasn't threatening me, treating me as a patient, but as a friend. As if we'd just been to the pictures together, sitting in the same row.

'Like when you go to the pictures?' I said. 'When the lights go on and you can go outside for a smoke, and what you saw on the screen was only a film?'

'Something like that, Donald,' she said. 'Something like that.'

A few days later she came back and asked,

'Could I go on the round mile with you and Rover and Maisie and the herd one day?'

'Of course. Any time you want.'

'I'm off duty on Saturday. I presume you take them out then too.'

'Every day but Sunday. We rest then.'

'I'll come Saturday.'

'Early. About eight.'

She was there waiting at the byre at eight. Rover made a great fuss of her, but Maisie and the herd saw nothing out of the ordinary. It was a good dry day, so she had no need of wellingtons or waterproofs. She was wearing a patterned jumper, and had her hair out, without the nurse's hat. It was curly brown. We walked slowly out through the wide wooden gate and across the yard to the field towards the rock where *Mac Talla nan Creag* lives. We didn't say much. Just watched the herd moving and grazing.

I sat in the hollow at the rock as usual and Nurse MacLeish sat on a small folding stool she carried in her rucksack.

'It's so quiet,' she said. 'Not a breath of wind. Nothing.'

'That's a big word,' I said. 'Nothing.'

She looked embarrassed.

'I don't mean "Nothing",' she said. 'I mean there are no cars or people or noise or anything.'

'But listen,' I said.

And I stood up and shouted into the rock,

'*Madainn mhath.*' ('Good morning.') '*Ciamar a tha thu an-diugh a Dhomhnaill?*' ('How are you today, Donald?')

And Donald called back the same.

'Try it,' I said to Nurse MacLeish, and she stood up and called into the fissure,

'*Madainn mhath. Ciamar a tha thu an-diugh a Phaitrisia.*'

And her voice came back, echoing through the morning's silence. So, he played the game with her too. He could be anyone. The rock cannot contain him, just as my body cannot contain all I think. I am in the rock and the rock is in me. Sometimes I have to lie down and sleep. I sleep best on Saturday night. That's when I let things go and cease clinging to them and I stop being a rock and become soft and pliable like a baby. I listen to the wind, which is the sound of the fairy folk out gathering bog cotton to keep them busy making clothes all winter long. I'm now at an age where I get up to go to the toilet twice a night. On clear and windless nights I go outside to pee and watch the stars twinkling above and listen to all the villagers snoring away in the dark.

But now all I hear is the hum of a distant wind turbine.

We walked on to the old peat-bogs, where Mary Ann usually appeared. Though not that day. She was always a shy girl and must have stayed well hidden behind the bogs. But the fairies weren't so shy. When we approached, we heard the noise but then, as always, they went quiet – for longer too, because they must have known there were two of us – but then resumed their cèilidh, singing and dancing and whistling far below.

Or maybe it was just me. I don't know, for Nurse MacLeish asked me, 'What's that tune you're whistling?'

And I said, 'I don't know. I only whistle it here, and I don't know the name of it, but when I leave I always forget how it goes until I'm here again.'

'It's a beautiful tune,' she said. 'I'll try and remember it.'

But she couldn't either, when I asked her later about it. And we walked on with the herd to *Lòn a' Phùinnsein* and she asked to borrow my stick so she could help guide the cows away from the danger areas, and from there on to *Loch na h-Eala*, where she too looked in the mirror of the loch and saw her image coming and going.

'Goodness,' she said. 'I look so much like my mother when I see my reflection in the water. And, if truth be told, like my granny. She was such a sweet woman. She knitted socks and jumpers and scarves and bonnets. I'm wearing one today. This beautiful Fair Isle jumper. She used to knit as she walked along.'

We listened to the birds singing at *Cnoc nan Òran* and had our lunch, and then walked over to the ruins where Catrìona and Eòghainn stay. Nurse MacLeish saw the remains of the cottage from a distance and said,

'I've never been out here. What a bonnie place it would have been to stay.'

And she ran towards it like a young girl and went inside. Next thing, there she was standing at the open window, her arms folded and leaning on the sill, just as Catrìona always did, looking out towards the horizon where I stood. And as I approached, she dipped back inside and sat where the hearth would have been and said to me as I came in where the door would have been,

'What a lovely house this would have made. The stove would have been there and here the kitchen table.'

We could almost smell the scones on the griddle and hear the porridge bubbling in the pan. And then she began singing,

> *'Pill iù Pill ill ill ill Eòghainn*
> *Pill iù Pill ill ill ill Eòghainn*
> *Pill iù Pill ill ill ill Eòghainn*
> *Pill ill èadhainn pill ill ill o h-eòin ...'*

'I took piping lessons when I was younger,' she said. 'From Calum Johnston. He was a patient teacher, and that was his favourite tune. It's the only one I remember.

> *'Pill iù Pill ill ill ill Eòghainn*
> *Pill iù Pill ill ill ill Eòghainn*
> *Pill iù Pill ill ill ill Eòghainn*
> *Pill ill èadhainn pill ill ill o h-eòin...'*

The pattern continued for the rest of the day. Whatever I heard, Nurse MacLeish heard too, though in a different way, and whatever I saw she too saw, in her own particular way. There was a world to share even if she saw it one way and I another. For once one step is taken, the next follows naturally. The way Maisie's left foreleg inches forward first, then the back right leg, then the front right and the back left, step by step, onwards, inch by inch, through the sparse grass.

10

THE STANDING STONE marks the halfway point of my daily journey. When Maisie sees it, she goes up and rubs herself against it and turns inwards, knowing she's on the way home.

There are all kinds of speculations about the standing stone. That it was built by the Druids. Or the Picts. Or the Vikings. That it was in homage to some pagan god, or marked the exact spot of the summer solstice, or where children were sacrificed at Lughnasa or maybe Samhain. Some say it was old men and women they sacrificed, as an official way of getting rid of burdens on the community. As if things are any different nowadays.

I think it was just put up as a basic shelter from the wind by a herdsman centuries ago. For the wind is fierce at this point. It comes at you straight from the north in all its bitterness and cold, and any shepherd lad or lassie with any sense would have put this stone up to shelter from the storm. All the rest is mumbo-jumbo.

North is bad. I tell you that. Cold and bitter. No one builds their house facing north, and if you study hens like I do, you'll find they always stick their heads first thing in the morning out of the hole that faces south in the coop, towards where the wind is warm. We had an engineer from Somerset on the boat when I was at sea. The North Eye he called the Evil Eye. West is where all the good things come from – the fish from the sea, the hay and oats and potatoes and carrots and cabbages from the machair and the North Atlantic Drift which keeps us from freezing. All the gravestones face east, because that's where Christ will come from on the day of the Resurrection.

The standing stone faces east and west with its thinner sides to the north and south. There are faded inscriptions to the east side, which no one has ever made out because they are in symbols no one can interpret. Of course there have been so many attempts, some experts calling it Ogham and others Pictish, though they bear no resemblance to other pre-Christian stones found elsewhere, from Callanish to Stonehenge and beyond.

Maybe they have no meaning, though the search for meaning goes on. Perhaps a shepherd lad idly scratched the pictures with a flint or stone, though I don't believe anything is ever just done idly. I go to the toilet for a reason and whenever I lift a stone or spade or stick or anything I do it for a reason: to weigh a bit of tarpaulin down or to dig a ditch or to move Maisie along. And if a Druidic priest, or his servant, carved the symbols he would certainly have done so with meaning if not conviction.

Maybe that line means the path ahead, and the curved bit above it the moon, and the two square shapes beside it are Donald and Mary Ann from two thousand years ago after they'd kissed and got married? Or maybe the line is this path I now walk every day with my cows and the curved bit above is the horn of some ancient Maisie and the two square shapes the fields where they grazed. We all put our own shape on the world. Fat people draw fat people and thin people thin people.

If I was to draw the world I would make it a perfect circle. Ice and polar bears would be all over the north. Sailing ships and whales in the east. Cowboys and cattle in the west. Sun and palm trees in the south. And God in the centre because without Him everything would dissolve. Sometimes I'm tempted to draw that on the standing stone, but that would be sacrilege, to carve over someone else's work, so maybe I should get another stone from up the hill and haul it down here and put my drawing on it. I could use chalk, but that would just wash away in the rain, so I'd use a chisel and a mallet and it would last forever and then, sometime in the future, another Donald could sit here too and wonder what it all meant. For the thing is that the past has as many mysteries as the future.

Donald John MacPherson was in school with me, and he was known as 'Nor'-West' because he did everything by the compass. Even out in the playground when we played football. If anyone was taking a penalty or a free kick, he'd always say, 'Hit it from the nor'-west of the ball and it will be sure to land in the sou'-east corner of the goal.' He joined the Merchant Navy and became a renowned skipper with the Blue Star Line on the South China run.

Most of the goals were scored in-off-the-post or in-off-the bar, though there were neither posts nor a bar, but two jackets or two jumpers thrown on the ground six feet apart. We judged by eye and lie and hope, which led to endless arguments that still go on whenever we meet.

The sun turns towards the west as I sit at the standing stone. Afternoon is here. I take my lunch. A mutton sandwich and a ham sandwich and my flask of tea. The mutton and tea always tastes better out of doors. It's a big flask, containing five cups. I have one in mid-morning when I stop at the loch, three here at the standing stone and then one later on in the afternoon on the way home. By that time it's lukewarm, but it's still tea. It's good strong tea, as good as a meal in itself. I boil it last thing at night and then leave it to stew in the pot until morning when I heat it up again before putting it into the flask. I like watching the kettle boil on the stove, especially towards the end when the steam rises from the spout and it whistles. Every time it boils it's like another mystery solved. The mutton is from Janet Smith's flock, though the ham is from the shop. While I eat, the cows chew the cud. I wonder if monks are allowed to eat mutton pieces. I suppose in some orders they are. So here I am in the middle of the five thousand all eating together out on the moor.

And I see that the standing stone marks time as well as space. For if it wasn't there I wouldn't know where I was. Well of course I would know where I was, but I wouldn't know I was exactly *here*. I know the contours of the land here and the shape of the grass and stones, but if the stone had not been erected by an ancient shepherd lad I would probably never have stopped here on my daily round and seen the world as I do, leaning against it. I can tell the time by the way the sun's shadow rests on the stone.

There are so many different ways to see the world. Sitting here, leaning against the stone, is one way, but when I stand up it's different, because I'm higher, and naturally it also all depends if I sit on this side of the stone or the other, because from this side I see the sea and from the other side the mountain.

'Do you have any hobbies?' Nurse MacLeish asked me the other day. 'Pastimes, I mean.'

And I was tempted to say I was too busy to have any hobbies or pastimes. Just customs and habits, though that's not true. I love looking at maps. I spend all my winter evenings studying them. Och, I know it's not like the old days when we all used to gather at Aonghas Fhionnlaigh's house and tell stories and sing songs and all that stuff, but that's long gone, so I just sit by the fire and work my way through Bartholomew's Atlas from 1942. It's the only one I have, and why should I buy or get an updated version? This is the one I know and am familiar with. It's my friend. I recognise places and countries that are now long gone.

On clear and starry nights, I go outside and gaze up to the heavens. I know the names of many of the stars in Gaelic: *An Reul-Iùil, Reul na Maidne, An Corg, Slighe na Bà Fèinne* and so on, but there are so many on different nights and different seasons that my knowledge is just a puddle. There's the Milky Way, which we call *Slighe na Bà Fèinn*, the Path of the Cows of the Fingalians. Even in the highest heavens, the cows make their way home in the dark. The *Grioglachan* (The Seven Sisters) – the mother cow and her six daughters – forever leading us to comfort on clear winter nights, with the red eye of *Aibhseag* in the endless field of *An Tarbh* (Taurus) following their grazing path across the heavens.

We're not afraid of the dark. I suppose because we're used to it. It's when I've learned most, standing outside there in the dark knowing how small I am in the universe. How alone I am and how much I miss my mother and grandfather and those quick daft days of my childhood when we played marbles and chuckies and football and how much I am the dark and need, despite myself, to hear and see Janet cackling to her hens in the morning and that teacher driving by playing his music, which is not mine. It may be that Janet Smith with her hens is the best thing we have. The last of the old native tribe. She's the only one around here who still measures distance by sound. Her mile limit is where she can hear the cockerel crowing from the barn door. It's only recently I've realised the hens gather round her not to be fed, but to hear her singing and talking. I don't think she has any idea I can hear her on windless days, telling everything to the hens. Or that she cares if I do. For who doesn't want to tell someone what they've heard and hope and fear, even if the response is only

'Cluck Cluck Good Luck' from a half-a-dozen hens?

Miss Smith is the only one here who still cuts the hay with a scythe, spitting on her hands to prevent blisters as she does it. She cuts and spreads and rakes and turns and gathers the hay during the last three weeks of August and into the first weeks of September, and by the end of the month they're in small stooks in her yard, wrapped with twine. She uses it to feed her sheep in the winter and to make nice beds for her hens.

I shouldn't really be calling her Janet Smith anyway. That's just her English name and I've never known her as that, but as *Seònaid Alasdair 'ic Sheumais Dhòmhnaill Fhionnlaigh* (Seònaid daughter of Alasdair son of James son of Donald son of Finlay), for in the old days if you shouted for 'Donald' or 'Janet' hundreds of them would arrive from all the villages over the brae as on the day of resurrection, so you had to distinguish them by their *sloinneadh* (genealogy) or individual ways – *Dòmhnall Dubh* (black-haired Donald) or *Seònaid Bhàn* (fair-haired Janet) or *Seònaid Bheag* (little Janet) or *Seònaid Mhòr* (Big Janet) or whatever trait might separate one Janet from another when they appeared on the horizon carrying their baskets of eggs or sacks of potatoes or creels of peats on their shoulders while knitting a shawl and singing an old waulking song. It's simpler nowadays, because all these people have gone and everyone's got shorter names anyway like Kylie or Chloe and Liam or Ryan.

I can only see the Northern Heavens, and though they're shining bright down where my cousins George and Angus and Murdo live down by Australia, I can't see the stars of the Southern Heavens. It's like being in a bedroom with two windows, one on this side where you can see the machair and one on that side where you can see the moor. But that's only a dream of mine, for my bedroom has only the one small skylight window where I can see the stars on a clear night. I think how the smallest star in the sky is bigger than our planet. Nothing separates me from God at those times. Nothing comes between us, because the stars are his too, and no one, not even Janet Smith, gets in the way because she, like everyone else, is in bed. When I see smoke curling from her chimney early every morning I'm glad she's still with us. Nights are so quiet. They never mean anyone any harm. Everyone breathes as they sleep, but that's permitted because that's not an ungodly noise. If a dog barks, whoever owns it silences it immediately. I can hear the port village in the distance. It has a different silence from everywhere else.

I like looking at the pages of the map that say World Geology and World Seismology because that's an unexplored world. For who wants to know what they understand already, like the ways of cows and sheep, when there are so many things I don't understand and wish I could. The World Geology page is all coloured in seven different shades to help me understand what things are made of. It says that all the yellow bits are Post Tertiary, the orange bits Tertiary, the green bits Mesozoic, the purple bits Palaeozoic, the pink bits Archaean Schists and Old Massive Crystalline, the red bits Younger Eruptive Rocks and the few white bits are Uncertain. I know the names of every field and hill and hollow and glen and rock and stream and river and loch here, so that nothing is uncertain. It must be exciting to be a mapmaker and discover and explore places that are unknown and uncertain. I wonder what they were called before the mapmaker arrived? Probably *Lòn a' Phùinnsein* and things like that. Though you can also discover and explore places you know already. It's what I do every day, because they're different every day depending on whether it rained overnight or whether the geese have already flown south and the first flecks of snow are already on the hilltops, when they weren't there yesterday. Wintry showers come in from the east and then sweep on.

So, of course, that leads me on to what all these words and terms mean, which means I have to take out a dictionary to find out that Palaeozoic, for instance, are rocks that were formed 538.8 million years ago, which is such a long long time ago. I doubt even Adam was around then. I think he was created much later, once things had settled down a bit and there was proper dust and air and water and things. So, I turn to the World Seismology page which shows me where all the earthquake and volcanic regions of the world are, though none of them are near me. There are sixty-two active volcanoes, the three nearest to me being in Iceland.

'I just look after my cows,' I said to Nurse MacLeish, and she nodded. 'But I like looking at maps.'

'Interesting,' she said. 'What about activities with other people?'

'I go to church,' I said.

'And do you stay for tea or a chat or anything like that?'

'No. I just go there and then come home. I dress up nice, and then put my other clothes on, even though it's Sunday. Maisie and the herd still need looking after on the Sabbath.'

'I see.'

'I study the seas,' I then added.

'The seas?'

'Aye. You know, the oceans and rivers and streams and lochs and all that. I like looking at them on the maps and learning all their names.'

'The Atlantic,' she said. 'The Pacific, the Indian and the Arctic. I remember learning the list in school.'

'Yes, and the Nile, the Amazon, the Yangtze, the Mississippi-Missouri, the Yenisei, the Yellow River, the Ob, the Rio de la Plata, the Congo and the Volga. The ten biggest rivers in the world.'

But she wasn't that interested and didn't give me a chance to tell her about the Tyrrhenian Sea and the Ionian Sea and the Ligurian Sea where I'd sailed long ago. There are so many things you want to say and can't because of that look in their eyes that says they're not interested and that you are boring them to death. What do they care about mastitis in cows and sheep flux and the way you tie a fisherman's knot to bind down the thatch in a wild winter's gale or the hopes I have for the future?

Despite our journey round the mile, she started giving me tablets.

'To calm your nerves,' she said.

Though I never take them, I keep them in the back of the cupboard in the scullery, for it's a sin to throw everything out. But she has also given me something I do use.

'Why don't you try one of these?' she said, giving me a small metal device. 'It's an iPod. A bit old fashioned now, but still working perfectly. It's the one I used to use. It has music as well as voices and visions as you go round.'

'I like old fashioned things,' I said to her.

She showed me how it worked.

'I've put music on I think you'll like,' she said.

And I do. Hank Williams, Jim Reeves, Rosemary Clooney, Calum Kennedy, Philomena Begley, The Beatles. Gregorian Chants from the monks of the Abbey of St Solemnes in France. I like that, though my favourites are Simon and Garfunkel. I especially like that song about the poor boy who never gets to tell his story. I've surprised myself. Nurse MacLeish also put on classical music that I love. I especially like Delius. When he comes on, I take the plugs out of my ears so that Maisie and the herd can hear him too. I've tried the others, but he's the only one they like.

And no wonder, for it makes us all feel big and free and spacious and dreamy when the orchestra plays 'On Hearing The First Cuckoo in Spring'. Even in midwinter, when that comes on, we are all back in the first day of

May – *Latha Buidhe Bealtainn* (The Yellow Day of Beltane) hearing her call from the small copse of trees. It's a joy to have all these voices from elsewhere join those of Maisie and the herd and *Mac Talla nan Creag* and Catrìona as we walk the round mile together. I think of how big a world lots of little things make. Like how I make my porridge every morning from a handful of pinhead oats and milk and watch how it bubbles up and swells to fill the pan and my plate and belly. One thing becomes another.

Last night I lay awake for a while listening to the sound of the sea through the open skylight window. I sleep upstairs because I can see further from there. On wild winter nights I watch the winds. There are twelve of them, coming from all points of the compass, and each comes in a different colour. The north wind is *dubh* (black), the one from the east *corcair* (purple), the south wind *geal* (white) and the west wind *odhar* (pale). Between the north and east are two winds, *breac* (speckled) and *dorcha* (dark), between the east and south *buidhe* (yellow) and *dearg* (red). Between the south and west winds are the *glas* (grey) and the *uaine* (green) winds, and between the west and north winds come the *ciar* (dark-brown) and the *liath* (blueish-grey) winds.

You never see them blowing in multi-colour together, though I have seen the *breac* and the *dorcha* and the *dubh* and the *corcair* all blowing at once like the ribbons on Mary Ann's hair flapping in the wind on an autumn day.

I watch the stars from bed. These are the Boisdale stars, and if I wake and stand up and look out the window I can see the sea surging in from the west. As a child, I was always told to close the west window at night because that's where the fairies came in, but I never closed it because I always wanted to see them, all green and silver and white, whistling and singing and piping and dancing their way through the night. I was an only child, and they were my friends. Able to do all the things I wished to do some day, dancing and singing and stealing the goodness out of the milk just to annoy people. I could be a spark of light in the dark or a sprite in the night to frighten people. Best of all, they could probably play football forever and ever without getting tired or having to do chores or getting called home for their tea. I'd be different now if they hadn't been there.

All I see now are the house lights blazing in the dark. Nobody sleeps well. Everybody is up watching some machine or lying in bed awake, worrying. Because they don't work hard enough. Never go outside, even for a walk. I don't see any of them all day long. I think they're afraid of being outside because they can't control it with a switch.

I never close the window and can hear the seals singing in the dark. I sing quietly back to them, so that no one but them can hear me through the open window. For a while there I wasn't sleeping well either. Had nightmares. Trapped in a maze or lost in long unknown corridors without a door. So I started saying 'Sweet Dreams, Donald' before I went to sleep, and I don't have them now. Just nice ones. Last night I was fishing with a silver rod out on the hill loch on a summer's evening, with a basketful of trout at my feet, and two of them sizzling away on the open fire beside me with four machair potatoes wrapped in foil cooking beside them.

11

AFTER THE STANDING stone there is a big wide open space which I dread to cross, because that's where I see the future, and I'm not in it. Maisie and the herd don't fear it, so either they can't see it, or do and they don't bother about it. They graze on. I can't comprehend this place without me. Who will look after Maisie and the herd? I'm the only one who keeps cows around here now anyway. The rest of the crofts are more or less tourist businesses, with pods at every corner. Will I join Mary Ann over there in the peat bogs, calling out in the hope that someone walks by to hear me and speak to me?

'You don't need to explain yourself, Donald,' Nurse MacLeish said. 'Because none of us can.'

I think she believes in me. That what I do every day is true, and as necessary as eating. Last week she said, 'I do yoga. Down at Julie's place. Every Monday and Thursday evening.'

'What's that?'

I knew what it was, but I asked her anyway. Maybe she was tempting me.

'Stretches and exercises. We do stretches for half an hour, then sit cross-legged for half an hour and say

"Ohm". Calms us all down.'

'Hmm.'

This is where the spaceport will be. Council development officers and a company from the mainland have already staked the ground out and are now in the process of buying the area by compulsory purchase. Some things are too important to be stopped. I objected, just as I did against the wind farm, but that was overruled because the authorities said I had my own croftland and that there was still plenty of common grazing land for the few cows I have, since no one else uses it anyway. But above all else, apparently, the development is needed for economic reasons. Otherwise, they say, unemployment will continue to rise, young people will continue to leave, and this place will become a wasteland. That's according to the local paper anyway.

It's not the spaceport I see, but a series of glass buildings. Which doesn't greatly concern me because glass houses are all over the place already anyway. Once upon a time people built little houses with hardly any windows because they wanted to shelter from the wind and rain, but now that galvanized and triple-glazed glass has been developed, everyone builds for the view. You can sit by the fire and watch the rain and wind and hail and snow and storm without getting wet or cold or blown over. It's pleasant, like watching television. It's a wonderful thing to stand at a big window and look out and see things, because in my grandfather's time the houses only had tiny openings and people just sat inside in the dark complaining or telling stories.

No. It's that there are no sheep or cows or hens or pigs or dogs or humans to be seen in or around the glass buildings. Either they're inside in good barns and rooms or they don't exist at all. The lawns are bright green with no dung or hoof marks or anything. What is land without footprints or plough rigs or sheep or cattle grazing on it? It doesn't smell of anything. Not of fresh-cut grass or petrol fumes from a mower or paraffin fumes from a tractor or anything. I walk around there every day and the smell of seaweed in the air vanishes as soon as I reach that patch and it becomes – not airless, but smell-less, if there's such a word. It feels like a lie, though no one has done anything wrong.

Nobody walks around and I never see anyone inside the glass buildings either, though shadows move about. So there's life. Maybe they're robots, I don't know. Which is one way of knowing, grandfather said. You know by the look of a thing what it's about. A nice fat healthy cow or a thin sickly one. Although I can't see into the fairy hollow I know it's a happy place. Yet though I can look all the way through this glass building and see nothing fearful, I know it's sad. Some houses, even when they're ruins, look happy, and others, even though they're brand new, look sad. It's something inside them. Maybe it's because there are no children around.

Sometimes you can't choose what happens to you. All you can do is try to get through it. The trick is to get out before you're old and wizened. I know a woman in Barra who got caught. She's called Flòraidh. One day she went out to tend the cattle, just like I do every day, and she too passed a fairy knoll on the way. But as she passed it, the knoll opened and the fairies got hold of her and took her inside. It was full of people, working and singing and dancing, and she was so happy to be there in their midst.

But when she made to leave, they said to her, 'Oh, no, my dear. You can't leave. You need to stay here with us.'

'I can't do that,' she said. 'I need to go back home.'

'Oh, you'll get home sometime later,' they told her. 'Stay and help us. And enjoy yourself.'

And this older fairy-woman said to her, 'You can go home when you've baked every drop of flour in that kist over there.'

'All right, then,' Flòraidh said.

So that very day she began baking. And every day she went back to the kist, it was as full as it was at the beginning. She became exhausted with it all, day after day. And one day she said to another fairy-woman, 'I'm exhausted. Baking bread every day, and yet every time I go to that kist it's as full as it ever was. And I can't get out of here until I finish what's in the kist.'

'Is that what they told you?' the woman asked.

'It is. When they took me in.'

'Well then, I'll tell you what you must do tomorrow. But don't let on I told you anything. When you've finished making your bannocks tomorrow, make sure that the rest of the flour you leave – what we call the *fallaid* (the leftovers) – make sure you return it into the kist. You haven't been putting it back into the kist, you're just throwing it away. But if you put the *fallaid* back into that kist every day, the contents will get smaller and smaller.'

And that's what she did. Every day, after baking the Bannocks, Flòraidh returned the *fallaid* into the kist. Then one morning, the kist was empty, with no flour left. So Flòraidh found the older fairy-woman and said, 'It's time now for me to go home. You said that I'd get home when I finished baking all the flour in the kist.'

'You will that,' the older fairy-woman said, 'when the kist is completely empty.'

'Well, then. You go and have a look. Every last grain of meal has been used up.'

'Has it?' said the woman.

She went over and saw not a drop of meal in the kist.

'I'm going home now,' Flòraidh said.

'Go,' said the woman, 'My blessing on you, but my curse on the one who taught you.'

They opened the fairy-knoll and let Flòraidh go. When she was outside, she looked about her and had no idea which way to go. She stood for a while and thought, 'I think this is the way I came, so I'll go this way.'

And she walked that way, down a familiar track toward a cottage in the distance with smoke coming from the chimney. It rose into the air like the sound her mother's songs made when she baked. Beside the cottage was an old ruin. It was where her house had been. Little children were running around the ruin. She went down and said to the children,

'Where do you stay?'

'In that cottage,' they said.

'Who's there just now?'

'Our mother,' they said.

Flòraidh went to the cottage and a woman came to the door. Flòraidh said to her, 'Do you know where the family who were in that house are? It's just a ruin now.'

'Oh, my dear,' the woman said, 'the folk who were in that house are long gone into eternity.'

'But that's the house I left. It's our house.'

'When did you leave, my dear?'

'Some days ago. I left to herd the cattle and the fairies took me in. I was in the knoll with them until now because they wouldn't let me out until I baked all the flour that was in the kist. And when I finished all the meal, they let me go.'

'Oh, my darling,' the woman said. 'If you've been in the knoll you've been there years and years, because it's many years since we came to live here. But you come in, and we'll look after you.'

And she went into the house.

'What shall I do?' Flòraidh asked. 'Since all my own people are gone.'

'Stay here,' the woman said. 'Stay here and we'll look after you. Stay here until my husband comes home and we'll see what he says.'

When he came home, his wife told him about Flòraidh and how she must have been years and years in the *Sìthean*.

'Well then, my dear,' the man said. 'It's years and years you've been in the *Sìthean*.'

'No, I don't think so,' said Flòraidh. 'I don't think it was that long. Just weeks.'

'It was years, my child. But I tell you this – since our own children are small they could do with someone of your wisdom to guide them and we could, no doubt, do with your help around the croft. You can work the land with us, if you want to stay here. It's your choice. And you can come and go as you please, whenever you want. The door is always open.'

I make scones every Saturday night to last me the week for pudding. I always leave the *fallaid* aside so as make the flour last longer. I've had the sack of meal now for well over a year. But you need to be careful not to let things get out of hand, because every morning as I cook my porridge I chant 'Cook, little pot, cook', but then always remember when it starts to bubble to say 'Stop, little pot, stop', in case it bubbles over and out the door and all over the island. It happened in a comic I read once.

After I stopped reading comics, I used to read the *Reader's Digest*. It was always full of stories about the future, and I hope that none of the stuff I'm seeing has anything to do with that. For they say that the things we see or imagine are only the distorted reflections of things we've heard or seen or read about throughout our lives. Which is why it's important not to read or hear or see anything except what your own eyes and ears see and hear. Especially for the first time, because then it's forever.

I know, for example, that *The Victor* comic and the

Reader's Digest and no doubt other comics and books all predicted that we'd be flying about in personal flying machines by now, which is ridiculous when we can't even get a bus once a week to the shop here. So I walk. You can walk everywhere here. You don't always have to be going somewhere in particular. There's no need for a car or a bus or a ferry or a plane unless you want things you don't need anyway. You can go anywhere in the world now without travelling anywhere. The best things in the shop are the corned beef tins. I like opening them with that magical small key, rolling the tin inch by inch. At first I was always cutting myself, but now I do it perfectly, rolling it back the way Mr MacNeill used to roll the strap back in school before placing it in the drawer for the next time. I give the contents to Rover who wolfs them down, and I keep all the tins to store things in. Nails, screws, nuts, bolts, needles and threads, and tars and creams for wounds in the herd.

I wonder why the past and future are so different from one another. The things I see in the past are fuller and fatter, as it were, and these things I see in the future are thinner and stringier. It's probably only because the older I get the thinner and stringier I've become myself. It's not that I've tried to lose weight or anything, it's just that I'm getting thinner. My biceps are smaller, my thighs and legs skinnier, and my face, when I catch myself in the mirror, has become gaunter. I'm turning into my grandfather all those years ago. Not just physically. Rover senses the fragility, now sitting nearer me, looking at me sadly. I'm getting to be the same age as him, in dog years. He's at rest, though he'd rise ever so slowly, if I whistled the old tune. He always hopes. For a kind word, or a pat on the head, or a bone to chew on. Saves me from hopelessness, and every day gives me courage. We've become one another.

'Being here together is enough. Isn't it, Rover, my dear?'

The things I see in the glass village look emaciated and – how shall I put it? – more insubstantial than the things I see in the fairy hollow or over at the loch, for instance. There, the water-lilies are fat and in full bloom, whereas the thin flowers I see growing inside the glass houses are tall and lifeless. Maybe they're plastic. I don't know. There are so many things I don't know. I wonder if they fight down in fairy-land like we do here? Over flags and things. I know they argue at Samhain, but I suspect that's just because of having too much to drink.

When I was younger I felt sorry for them because they never left home or went ploughing or down to the machair to play football or anything, but now I admire them, forever self-sufficient, never having to go to the shops for bread or newspapers or toilet paper, or out to work in the wind and rain, but living quietly here with everything to hand, from tiny dancing shoes to rows of silver reeds for their pipes. Everything changed when the fairy knoll became an ordinary mound of grass you could plough or walk on. It was as if we'd thrown away our best story, where everything we'd ever dreamed or imagined had taken place. It had all come to nothing, except for fragments of songs and unbelievable stories and folk saying 'that's where they lived in the old days'. I didn't want it to be nothing, because they were part of us, and if they were nothing, so were we.

I was only allowed in once. It was a still, moonlit night. I went out to check that the gate between the sheep fank and the stream was closed. It was. As I walked back, I saw the light flickering over towards the hollow, and at first thought it was just the will-o-the-wisp, which is common on clear cold nights. But it felt different. These weren't haphazard windy lights but deliberate ones, the way we used to put on the mast lights when sailing through fog in the Bristol Channel.

So I walked towards them and as I walked they kept their distance, the way I do with the cattle, and they do with me, knowing that I will follow in due course. The hollow opened up and stairs led down with the light ahead, dropping step by step, until I found myself in a lamplit room smelling of peat fire with the shadows of the flames flickering on the earthen walls. Things without shadows are dead, so everything here must be alive.

I looked around. A woman was baking bread on a griddle in the corner. Every time she finished a loaf she gathered the leftover flour in her apron and put it back into the kist. You should never let anything go to waste. It would be her salvation.

Half a dozen little wizened old men were working at looms and anvils and creels while in the centre of the room a dozen green-kilted women were waulking the cloth and singing while children wheeled around, flying about the place as they pleased. I stood by the little cobbler for a while watching him fashioning the most delicate leather shoes on the tiny last. They were green with yellow soles, and his neighbour on the spinning wheel was making the loveliest of laces for him out of bog-cotton, which the cobbler fitted into the shoe tongue holes with a slender needle. And here's the thing: every time they used a tool, whether a needle or a hammer or a saw, the tool became the perfect shape for the material being worked. Round when they had to cut round a corner, so small as to be almost invisible when they needed to insert it into a tiny space, and sharp or smooth depending on whether they were cutting wood or polishing a table. That's how work should be: the right tool for every occasion. Not like I've been, with blunt screwdrivers and unsharpened saws and broken sticks here and there, just making do.

'Perfect,' the cobbler said, as he finished polishing the leather, lifting up the two tiny shoes and showing them off to me with delight. A child ran over and put them on her feet and skipped away with joy.

Maybe it's because we can be children and old men at the same time. I'm not sure whether I became smaller while in the knoll or they became larger, but we were the same size. We were all human. Or superhuman. One of the women who'd been waulking the cloth came over to me and curtsied and took my hand and led me across the floor in a waltz to the music of a fairy-woman sitting on a wooden milk churn playing the accordion. I can't remember the tune, but I know the woman who danced with me had green eyes and freckles. I'm not a good dancer, but that evening I danced like a child. I suppose because she led me and I just did every step she did. She let go of me and led me over by the fingertips towards another space where the fire was.

Everything was the same in the knoll as it was up here above, except brighter and quicker and happier and lighter. I think that if the little people weren't similar to us and the pots and pans and scythes and stoves they used weren't the same as ours, we'd never see them at all.

The red glow came from an old Rayburn Stove. My mother stood stirring a pot while Grandfather sat on a three-legged stool by the fire, smoking his briar pipe. He was cutting up a wedge of tobacco with the old red-handled knife he always had. He beckoned me to sit down. Mum poured out two ladlefuls of broth and gave me a warm cut of bread from the stove oven while Grandfather puffed away on his pipe. He hummed the tune he always hummed when happiest,

'Latha dhomh is mi Beinn a' Cheathaich
Air far a la lo ro ho bhi ho
Hoireann is o ho ri hi o ho...'

And Mum joined in the singing and me too, in between the mouthfuls of soup and bread. And we sang for ages and ages until Mum said, '*A Dhòmhnaill, thalla is faigh tuilleadh mòine son an teine.*' ('Donald, go and get some more peat for the fire.') She handed me the basket and I went out to the stack, climbing up the stairs led by the moonlight and filled the basket and turned to go back inside, to find myself at my own peat-stack with a basket in my hand and Rover by my side and the hollowed-out hill nowhere to be seen. I came into the house and put the peats on my own fire, which had almost died out, but kindled away as I laid them on the embers until they made a bright warm flame.

I keep the best peat-stack in the place. Not that it matters nowadays, for not many bother, since they have central heating. It's not a boast – just that I can't stand things being thrown together willy-nilly. Grandfather taught me how to build a proper stack, laying each peat at a slight angle from the bottom up, leaving room for the wind to breathe through, so that when the stack is complete it's straight and even and compact and secure.

'Ship-shape,' as Captain MacInnes used to say. 'Order, not chaos.'

The problem, of course, is that once you get organised something unexpected always happens and you're back where you started again. No sooner have I set up the bottom rows of the stack than one of Janet Smith's rams comes galloping over and charges my work on to the ground again. I drive him away with my stick and start all over again until the stack is all neat and complete. That takes weeks, in between my herding rounds.

Tourists stop in their cars when they see my peat-stack. They take pictures of it. 'It's like taking a photograph of a photograph,' one of them said to me once.

I have to be careful when to light the fire. There's

nothing better than lighting it on a winter's morning when it's frosty and cold, but though it's tempting to light it on a chilly Spring or Autumn morning, it's then so sad to let it die down to white ashes as the day gets warmer. It's best at these times just to light it when I get back home in the evening, tired as I am.

Here, Maisie and the herd graze on, their full fat bellies and udders swinging in the light breeze. I look forward to the warm glass of milk straight from the cow when I get home. I always squeeze the first creamy milk from the udder into a wooden pail my mother had and leave it until I've finished milking all the cows and then take that first pail with me into the kitchen.

I wash, sit at the kitchen table, and scoop the creamy milk out with a large mug and drink it. It's the best drink in the world. Sometimes when I take that first sip it reminds me of that first-ever pint of Guinness I drank in a grubby dockside pub in Dublin before I went to sea. Where I soon learned that it was not for an obsessive man like me.

I keep seven cows for a reason: the lean years and the fat years. Joseph and the Pharaoh with his dream of seven lean cows eating seven fat cows. Abundance and famine, the priest said, and asked us to prepare for the hard times to come.

I don't know if I have. I know next to nothing, which is probably better than knowing everything. Maybe I've wasted all those years. Maybe Nurse MacLeish will tell me, if I ask her. I won't. What have I had anyway? When Grandfather, and then Mother, died, I was left alone, with everything. Thirty hens, twenty sheep and twelve head of cattle. A house almost falling in on itself and a good byre. The byre is as good now as it was then and the house better. I reduced the hens to ten, and the sheep to twenty before giving them over to Janet Smith. She makes a bit of a living selling hens. Takes the eggs and puts them in her east-facing window where the sun hatches them. She says it's what the lapwings do, laying their eggs on the morning side of the hill. I've always kept the cattle to the golden seven. Maisie, five heifers and a bullock. It's enough. Everything doesn't have to be profitable to be useful.

'Are you sure it's seven cows you have?' Nurse MacLeish asked me. 'I'm sure I sometimes see more. Sometimes less. Everyone says the same.'

'It's how people count,' I said. 'Folk sometimes see things.'

God only knows what will happen to them once I go. Poor things. I wonder if there will be a place in heaven where I can keep a herd. If not, I'm not sure it's worth going there. Surely there will be, for all the great men of history were pastoralists and shepherds. Abraham and Isaac and Jacob and King David and of course the great Shepherd himself. Surely there will be pastures green for Maisie and all of us, as promised?

I think of these things as I cross the spaceport with my herd, my heart in my mouth. I wonder if I could avoid the space, but I can't, for that would be to break the magic circle and rework a path which would take us years and years to get accustomed to. And, besides, it wouldn't be right or fair. You've got to take the good with the bad. Otherwise, you're a coward.

It's strange how we always want to fill space. If there's an empty shelf in the house I stick cups or pans or something on it, and then outside if there's an empty place someone puts a tractor or a shed or sheep into it. But what if the space is already taken, and we block the way for the *Sluagh* (the Host of the Dead) who travel about at night or the spirits who use that space as their road between heaven and earth? Oh, I know they say they can probably travel through things, but still it would be awkward for them. That's why there are open spaces in the first place and why putting large windfarms or spaceports on them is wrong. The spirits will remember it all, and obstacles will come our way in return because of it. You see, this is what I think: space is not just like an empty milk bucket waiting to be filled. It's already full of air and atoms and angels and all kinds of other invisible things.

The thing is, Maisie and the herd could easily do the circuit on their own. They don't need me. They know it better than I do. Where to go and where to pause and where to stop and where to drink and where to graze and where to stand and stare. They could do all that themselves, avoiding *Lòn a' Phùinnsein*, finding their own slow gentle way home at the end of the day, and I could meet them in the barn and feed them and milk them and lay them down to rest and chew the cud and sleep.

But it gives me something to do all day long. The

chance to take care of them. It's nice to be able to care for something, to look after something precious. Something to love. There, I've said it. It's a word that was never spoken in our house. In our family. Or in the community, as everyone keeps calling it. I don't think I've ever heard anyone say 'I love you' to anyone else around here. They probably thought it was like a sack of potatoes and if you used the words too often you'd then run out of them. Och, I've heard folk say '*Is toigh leam thu*' ('I like you') loads of times, but that's not the same, is it? Liking and loving.

I mean, I like my shoes and my white shirt and tie for Sunday, but I wouldn't say I love them. Same with hate. Folk say 'I hate this, I hate that and I hate the other', but they really don't. They just dislike it, like homework. And what is this love we all talk about? Archie MacTavish in the next village was always considered strange because they said he loved his wife so much that he almost told her about it.

Mum loved me. I know that, though she never said it in words either, and I suppose that day Mary Ann kissed me was the nearest I came to it. It was warm and tender and happy, but most of all it was this – it took me out of myself. That's it. For that moment – these moments – I wasn't myself. I became someone else. It must be what a caterpillar feels like the moment it turns into a butterfly.

I could have loved the whole world at that moment. Given my shoes, my clothes, my hair, my life, to anyone who asked for them because they meant nothing to me compared to being so near Mary Ann. Maybe that's what the priest means when he says that God is love and that he so loved the world that he gave his one and only son that we might not perish but have eternal life. For you will give everything you have when you are in love. Your goods and chattels and hopes and dreams and everything.

I would do that for Maisie and the herd. I really would. If they were in danger or kidnapped, I would exchange my life for them. They speak like me. Their moos are soft and stretched out and I notice this most when I take them north to market where their lowing becomes quicker and more anxious, just like my voice does, rushed by all those other buyers and sellers and drovers and cattle being driven into their pens and the auctioneer who speaks ever so fast. Of course I understand that part of it is just the stress of the crowded market, but it's more than that, for when we find a quiet corner and settle down and a drover from the mainland comes over and speaks to me in an Invernessian accent, all drawling and sort of sing-song, Maisie and the herd begin to moo that way too for a while, as if they're hypnotized by the way the man speaks. I haven't tested it, but I wonder if cows abroad also speak in Irish or Swedish or Spanish accents. I bet they do. Mind you, when I was abroad at sea, I didn't speak with any of these accents. But I was only visiting, not a native.

Which makes me think how stupid Eòghainn was. Not that he didn't understand the poetry Catrìona spoke but that he didn't love her enough to overcome that riddle of language and distance and time. She could have chanted 'Skip to my Lou, Skip to my Lou my darling, be gone', and he should still have stayed there and joined her in the song if he loved her, instead of running away. And how she must love him, standing there day by day looking for the prodigal lover to appear on the horizon. If he were to appear, in rags, crawling on his knees, she would rush out of the ruins and greet him and shower him with kisses and put a ring on his finger and a cloak on his back and kill the fatted calf for him. She said that to me one sunny summer's morning.

Mum would do that for me if she could, but memory holds us all back. After a day's ploughing Dad was always tired, and though she would have liked to go out for a walk with him or sit by the fire talking, all he wanted was food and then to lie down and rest. There's a spider in the corner of the house, just up there between the stove and the kitchen door. I've watched him for hours weaving his web. Without any knitting needles or anything. And now he's resting, sitting in the centre, waiting for his dinner. Since Mum died I've always made my own.

I know, if she could, she would stay here until I came down and give me a long warm cuddle like when I was a child and make a good hearty breakfast for me before setting me on the way out to the moor with the cows, but she does the best she can, and each morning leaves that whiff of mint perfume that stays with me through the whole long day. That long cuddle she gave me some seventy years ago, the day I fell and grazed my knee, has kept me going ever since. It's gone by so quickly, even though I've done everything slowly.

I know where she gets the mint because we used to walk that way when I was small – it's down by the stream on the way to the church. When we reached there, she always picked a few leaves and crushed them in the palms of her hands and then caressed her face before tousling my hair with them so I too smelt of watermint the whole day long. Sometimes a fragrance matters more than anything. I can smell the seaweed from the back of my house and know that a good tide has brought in a whole pile of tangle to feed the early spring crops. I miss the things she had around the house – scented soaps, geraniums, her rosaries, those glass bottles that kept all kinds of sweet mysteries.

She took a risk being tender, for we were all supposed to be tough. To cope with the wind and the rain and the dark and the bare landscape and the poverty. If you were soft before all that harshness, you wilted and died. Gnarled hands and wrinkled faces proved you'd endured it all. Which is why everyone believed in fairyland and witches and goblins and the little people, who could come and help you with the harvest, though you'd have to make some deal with them in that underworld as here in the overworld. You could leave a glass of milk out by your door and sometimes that would suffice.

In this harsh environment, who would not wish for an alternative world? Who wouldn't hope for a white horse which could turn into a fairy lover and sweep you across the mountains? Or a seal who could be a glistening mermaid and bear you twelve children before she returned to the sea, and then sing mournfully for you every time you went down to gather the seaweed in your cart? Anything to get away from this dull, drab existence. Where none of your neighbours ever stole from you or committed any heinous crime: these were done by the bad fairies or the water-horse, though Seonaidh along the road was always implicated, for he had the evil eye, which could turn milk sour and cause Maisie to die without reason. Mum must have loved a lot to have resisted all that.

I pat Maisie on the rump to tell her I love her and she grunts her approval. We leave the spaceport and move on towards the site of *An Taigh Mòr* – The Big House – where, once upon a time, so many feasts and parties were held.

12

THE BIG HOUSE was built between 1820 and 1830 for Sir Archibald Sinclair. He bought the island after the collapse of the kelp industry at the end of the Napoleonic War, with the intention of turning the area into a sporting estate. It never worked.

The house is now owned by an American man who works for Microsoft, though he's hardly ever here. It's empty, though some friends of his come now and again in helicopters and stay for a week or so. At first Maisie and the herd were frightened by the noise, but they've become used to it.

I used to look through the windows to see what was inside, but it was just the usual stuff – big armchairs and sofas and clocks and huge pictures on the wall – so I stopped looking. Nothing ever moved in it. It just sits there silently as a mark of wealth or desire or something. It was once The Big House. It's now just the empty old one. The doors are locked.

No one locks their doors around here, except in those new holiday houses. Why on earth would they? It's not as if we have anything worth stealing – just the usual rubbish – so why bother? And what would a burglar or a thief do anyway with anyone's stuff? The land is so bare and open that everyone sees what everyone else is doing, so he could hardly creep in, even during the darkest night, and steal away with anything without everyone knowing. They'd hear him, because we hear everything in the dark.

And even if he did steal and get away, where would he take the stuff? There's no pawn shop and he'd be seen boarding the ferry. Nowadays he could sell the stuff on the internet, but who really would be interested in buying Janet Smith's hens or the only bit of jewellery she has in her house, an ear-shell from the shore her mother gave her when she was a child? It's her pride and joy and she's always going on about it, but no thief has yet been tempted by her boasting. She keeps all her worldly goods in a wicker basket hanging by a heather rope from the ceiling and whenever she needs money she stands on the small step-ladder I made for her and takes a handful of coins, crowns and sixpences and florins and farthings, and stuffs them in her pocket. All the shop-keepers accept them, telling her they'll be worth a fortune one day. In the olden days a cow was worth an ounce of gold, which wouldn't get you very far nowadays.

The treasures I have, apart from Maisie and the herd, are inside my head and can't be stolen. Well, I used to think that, but now know better. They're as stealable as cattle. A folklorist came round once and asked me for stories, as if they were sausages or sheep to be sold, rather than a thing to be shared on a dark winter's night when the wind is howling down the chimney and you want to frighten everyone with a ghost story which will linger even when the sun rises on a bright morning.

It's like milk too. I still drink it straight from the cow, though these days you're not allowed to sell it like that and it's weak and watery and pasteurized when you get it in the shop. Skimmed, with all the creamy goodness taken out of it. Sometimes I find myself telling a story in my head that includes something I heard on the radio or saw on television or read in a magazine and it's like a skimmed, spoiled story. We have begun to behave like strangers. Our stories don't match the way we walk anymore. They're too fast. Maybe they don't see me. The problem with going fast is that you're here one minute and there the next, so nothing between here and there really matters.

It's too sudden, and sudden changes don't do anyone any good. It takes from late April or early May through until September, or sometimes October depending on the weather and on what variety I've sown, for the potatoes to grow, and it takes time for a calf to become a cow, and a puppy to become a wise dog, and each stage is as important as the next. You can't rush by. I realise a caterpillar turns into a butterfly in an instant, but that's just from our way of looking at it. For the caterpillar it's been a whole lifetime and for the butterfly just a start.

Of course, cattle rustling was big business in the old days, when our wealth was measured by how many cows and bulls you owned. Not by peasants like me, who were only allowed by Sir Archibald to have one milch cow and calf, but by his lairdship and his kind. No wonder they could afford to have pipers and harpists and poets play for them and recite to them on their ramparts every day and then hold these huge feasts and parties in the evenings, while folk like me starved on scraps of shellfish from the shore.

So we too escaped into story and song. 'A cow will see you through the year, but a song or a story will take you to the ends of the earth,' they claimed, though I found the opposite: no one understood me beyond the threshold of my house.

'*An t-amadan ud.*' ('That fool.')

'*An gloic esan.*' ('Idiot.')

The folklorist who came to see me didn't show that much interest in me either, because all I had was what he called '*bloighean*' (fragments). I had the full things alright once upon a time, but how could I remember them all when there was no one to listen to them, and if there were, no one who understood? I recited them to Maisie and the herd for some years, but even they seemed not to hear them, so I sort of forgot them, for what's the point in telling a story if no one listens? The thing is, though, a wee part of a story or song is enough as long as whoever is listening knows what the rest should be. Like when I hear the words '*Beinn Dòbhrain*' (Ben Dòbhrain) I know it's not just referring to the mountain in Argyllshire, but to the great song composed by Duncan Ban MacIntyre in the 18th century where he praised the Ben as not just a wonder of nature but a place where he could get his dinner by going up and stalking a deer. I know all 653 lines of the song, which is composed in the form of a pìobaireachd, with its *ùrlar* (ground), then its *siubhal* (variation), then the *crùnluth* (finale), but I don't need do hear or carry the whole song to be climbing the Ben with Duncan, for as soon as I hear the first words, *An t-urram thar gach beinn aig Beinn Dòbhrain* (The honour about every mountain is Ben Dòbhrain's) there I am with Duncan watching the fawns *ris na laoigh bhreaca bhallach nach meathlaich na sianta le 'n cridheacha meara le bainne na cìoba gnoiseanach eangach le 'n girteaga geala le 'n corpanna glana le fallaineachd fìoruisg le faram gun ghearan feadh ghleannach na mìltich*.... all speckled and dappled that no tempests benumb their hearts being gladdened by milk of deer's hair grass, small-snouted and agile, with their little white haunches, their bodies made wholesome by salubrious spring waters, contentedly rustling through the glens of sweet grass...

The wee bit is always part of the whole, best world. I know, for instance, that if someone around here says 'Golden Wonders' he's not just talking in general about the best potato in the world, but about the floury local ones grown here on the machair and which are best eaten by hand with a plate of herring, with good salt butter slathering the potatoes, and always taken with a glass of fresh milk straight from the cow. That's what it means. If it doesn't mean all that and more, it's just a useless remnant, like the half-broken shaft of a spade, which folk then just throw away.

I wonder if a herdsman in Mongolia or Australia would understand me. I suppose so, because we're at the same trade, humming away in our deserts, so far away from each other.

So I clammed up. Locked the house, as it were, just like that American billionaire. who lives across the ocean while his goods and chattels gather dust in a faraway mansion.

I know Mr Haas. I've met him a few times, because every time he's here he always comes across with his visitors so they can get their photograph taken with Maisie and the herd to show their friends back home.

But the last time he was here, he came by to see me late in the evening before he left. He had a bottle of whisky in his hand.

'Would you mind,' he said, 'sharing this dram with me? That's the word, isn't it?'

'Indeed it is,' I said. 'Come in.'

He drank more than I did. I was careful to keep to one glass. He was good company. Talked about his people who had originally come from Armenia to New York in the late 1800s. Tailors, then clothing manufacturers and shopkeepers and owners, first in New York then in Colorado and Maine. His grandfather married a Scots emigrant woman, Helen Chisholm.

'Her family were cleared from the Highlands along with so many others. But she did fine. I remember her as an old lady in the nursing home telling me stories from here. Ghost stories and fairy stories, though she didn't call them that. Old tales, she called them.'

And he was good. Knew a few of them off by heart, though they sounded a bit made-up to me, with phrases I didn't recognise. But maybe that was just his American way.

'I hear tell you have some fine stories,' he said to me, and I just said,

'No. Not really. I only know about cattle and crofting.'

'You'd be big rancher over our way,' he said. 'Had you gone when younger.'

As he left, he muttered something about me going over to the Big House sometime and taking a look round if I wanted.

'Just to air it and keep an eye on things,' he said. I took it to be drink talking.

It wasn't. Some months later a letter arrived. I never get any letters. Well, apart from the electricity bill and circulars. So it was quite a memorable day when I found the air-mail envelope sitting behind the door when I came back from my round. It had a beautiful blue and red stamp of the Statue of Liberty and my hand-written name and address done with a blue-inked fountain pen. I know that because the steward on the last ship I sailed on used to show off his hand-writing in the same style. Cursive, he called it.

'Nothing to do with cursing,' he said. 'It just means rounded.'

It was a longish letter. It read:

Dear Mr MacDonald,
I often remember the evening we spent together
by the fire, and my apologies if I got a bit maudlin
from the whisky!

I don't know if you remember me suggesting that
you could take a look over the house sometime, and
what was a suggestion could now become a reality.
Sandra, the cleaner – you'll have seen her around
no doubt – has told me she wants to retire and, as
we talked back and forwards, she mentioned your
name and that you go past the house anyway on
your daily walk.

In short, would you consider taking on the role of
sort of handyman/caretaker for the property? Sandra
says she can still come by once a week or fortnight
to do the basic cleaning, but says that there are lots
of other more practical jobs that need done, and
suggested that you'd be perfectly able to do them.
Keeping the garden in shape and repairing broken
slates and windows and things that are open to the
elements that you know better than anyone else.

We realise you're busy with your herd, but
Sandra says they can more or less look after
themselves anyway. The thing is, Donald, I'm
not getting any younger myself and will likely be
coming over less and less. The family want me to
sell it, but I refuse. Over my dead body, as dear old
Mrs Chisholm-Haas was wont to say!

Increasingly, folk want to travel over there and
see some of the old things. You might consider acting

as a sort of 'cultural guide' for those visitors! I know fine that's not the kind of fancy language you'd want to use, Donald, but it's the kind of thing you'd do naturally. You're native to the place. You know all its history. You can do it in Gaelic if you want. And I know that the visitors would love to see their own half-forgotten dream made true. Sandra has kept the Highland things well-aired and free from moths etc in the dressing-room and – even if I say so myself, Mr MacDonald – you'd look absolutely splendid in the regalia I've left there.

Please do think about it. At the very least, take a look around and in the house, and you can let me know of things that need fixed or renewed or repaired.

Thank you, Sir, and I look forward to hearing from you sometime.

Slàinte!

Wendell Haas.

I didn't reply, but after a while thought the house looked so lonely and sad every time I passed it that I decided to look in.

It was seeing the Big House all locked up day and night with no one in it and even I not bothering to glance in through the windows any more that did it. 'That's me,' I said to Maisie one day, and she looked at me as if I was daft, but mooed in agreement all the same. I walked up to the front door and tried the handle and to my surprise it turned and opened. It had never been locked in the first place. Only rumour and belief had locked it.

The main hallway was large and filled with light from the east-facing windows. Enormous oil paintings decorated the walls: cattle grazing by dark blue lochs and ones of angels and cherubim and seraphim emerging over Mother Mary from bright blue skies. I always liked the wee fat cherubs with their chubby cheeks in the missal we used to have and I'm sure they still watch over me, because life has been so wonderful, with food always in the cupboard, Rover by the fire, Janet Smith singing away to her hens over the brae, and Maisie and the herd snorting and farting away to their hearts content in the byre.

'It's amazing to be alive,' as Roddy the Bosun said to me the morning after a heavy night's drinking in Auckland. Later, as we sailed round Cape Horn in a storm, we all heard him muttering as he struggled away on deck, *'Fuiling a bhugair, dh' òl thu d' oisglinn ann an Auckland.'* ('Suffer, you bugger, since you drank your oilskin away in Auckland.')

The big room on the right had a piano in the corner and of course I sat at it and played the only tune I learned at school all those centuries ago:

'Baa baa black sheep, have you any wool?

Yes, sir, yes, sir, three bags full.'

I was astonished that I could remember these sixteen notes, which I could never get beyond and still can't. It was out of tune.

And then I heard the birds. At first, I thought they

were outside, but the twirls and tunes were different. Sadder and lower and more apologetic than the curlews and oystercatchers and peewits I was used to outside. Laments rather than reels, songs of sorrow rather than joy. And I followed the sounds of the notes, down the stairs which led through the back of the house (where the original servants' quarters must have been) and then up a long winding steel stairway with the calls getting louder and louder and more lamentable as I climbed. They must have accepted their fate, or their songs would be cheerier.

Up there, in the attic, was an aviary, full of the most beautiful birds in the world with blue and red and orange and yellow and purple plumages, all of them flying around the golden cages, which lay open. I don't know for sure, but I thought they were nightingales and canaries and finches and ones like that, because I'd seen pictures of these kinds of birds in my school books. They were shocked at my sudden appearance and fled back into their cages, where they perched anxiously and stayed while I worked out what was happening.

What a system! There were sixty cages and sixty different birds, and a seed and water contraption tied to each cage from which the birds pecked at. And then, at the bottom of every cage, was a waste system so that all the bird droppings and effluent would wash away, so that the birds could stay there forever, if need be, while Mr Haas was away.

I wanted to open the skylight windows and release them all, but they were not mine, and I had no authority, so I left them there and went back down the stairs. As soon as I left, they resumed their mournful songs, which stayed with me all day long.

I opened the door and unsnecked the windows and let some air into the house, allowed the furniture to breathe. The oil painting of Sir Archibald sang in the dark and the bronze busts on the tables burst daily into flames and the heavy dusty curtains that hid everything away swayed in the gale-force wind raging in through the open windows.

The fire and grate were clean and empty, but I took in a stack of peat and put that in a basket by the fire and light it on cold winter days when I stop by. Folk think the house is now haunted and go around asking each other if they've seen lights on in the Big House and seen smoke coming out the chimneys. None of them have forgotten that there were fires before there were chimneys.

'He was such a wicked man, that Sir Archibald Sinclair,' said Janet Smith. 'Cleared all the people from the land and made a pact with the devil. No doubt that's the smoke from him burning in hell.'

The fire lit well because it was so well aired. All the bedrooms are upstairs, and I aired them all, though I never slept in them. That would be unseemly. The library was my favourite place because it is filled with maps. Not just in the books on the desks and on the shelves but all over the walls. Maritime charts, mostly, because Mr Haas also has a yacht in which he tours the world. So much open sea, but also so many rocks and reefs and winds and currents to contend with, from the

North Atlantic Drift near us to the Kurushio Current where east meets west.

I wrote to Mr Haas.

Dear Mr Haas,
I've looked into the house. It was unlocked. I'm really worried about the birds all caged in there. What do you want me to do with them?
    Yours sincerely,
    Donald Michael MacDonald

And he wrote back.

Dear Mr MacDonald,
Thank you so much for writing me to let me know about the house. I know it's unlocked.
    Please release these poor birds. I'm not sure if they will survive if released into the open, but do what you must. It was my son's idea and it has grieved me ever since.
    Wendell Haas

I asked Doctor Alick, and he suggested releasing them one by one over a period of time so as to not overwhelm the native birds, or vice versa. It would give each of them a chance to survive. Those who did were pleased, singing away on the rocks and moor and machair in their new world.

The freed birds have become my new friends. It's as if they're ever so thankful for being allowed to fly about in the open fresh air, but nevertheless they can't forget their old home, which was also their prison. I don't know. But I do know that they fly backwards and forwards from their new homes on the moor and on the shore to where they once stayed, where they hover over the roof for a while, as if unsure whether to go back in or to wheel away. And they always do, singing as they rise into the air.

I think they want me to care for the old house too, so I do. It's perhaps not even because Mr Haas asked me, but because they do, so I go along when I can to make sure the roof vents are opened and that the windows are dry and the doors open without squeaking as they did before and that the place is ventilated and smells of the birds' newly won air rather than the must of decay.

I can do some of that work as I take Maisie and the herd on their walk. They know how to graze beyond the walls and Rover sits there looking at them for a while, then looking across at me, as I stand on a ladder painting a gable window, or spraying one of the doors with WD40. I try to do most of the work outside, though sometimes I need to go inside the house to deal with the decay there.

And, daft as I am, I couldn't help but seeing myself as the big decayed house. Hidden away behind my poverty and my strangeness and my cows. My oddness and difference. And it wasn't even that I had hidden myself away, but that I had been hidden away by others. *Amadan. Gloic.* Smells of dung. Manure. Strange. So old-fashioned. And who does he think he is, anyway?

Something special, or something weird, raiking away out there on the moor every day muttering to himself and hearing things and seeing things that no one else can hear or see. Doesn't he realise we also see things and hear things and don't consider that strange? Yesterday, as I was passed the dog-rose bush I heard a humming. A bee was trapped inside the rose, which had closed its petals. I opened them up and let him free. If I hadn't been listening I would never have heard him.

All they have to do is ask, 'How are you, Donald?', and not just accept the usual answer, 'Fine, oh, fine', but instead hear a flood of language from the very depths of the Tyrrhenian Sea, a storm of translated speech, as if Maisie and the herd and Rover and Wilhelmina and Coinean and Eòghainn and Catrìona and the bees and the rocks and the earth itself have been given tongue.

'*How am I?* I'll tell you how I am. Heartbroken. For once upon a time, when I was young and easy under the apple boughs and happy as the grass was fairy green and Mum was walking about the house all covered in flour and singing and Grandfather was out in the byre milking the cows, I heard Mary Ann skipping along the road and chanting that rhyme about singing a song of sixpence a pocket full of rye, so I ran out to see her and when she saw me she did a somersault twice over ever so quick that I didn't even...'

And I stop there, because if I keep on going there will be no end to it and I will love everyone in the whole world so much that their indifference will break my heart again and the story will have no beginning or middle or end, as if that ever mattered. The story is always a beginning with no end. Some folk say that every moment is unique, but I'm not so sure. All mine live on daily, which is forever.

Nurse MacLeish helped me. She came and pushed open my unlocked door. At first, of course, I feared. All that dust and dirt and rubbish and garbage inside. All that quietness, with the caged birds mournfully singing up in the attic. Sometimes it's better not to sing.

'She'll think me strange.'

'Will certify me.'

'Literally lock me away.'

Instead, she listened. Oh my God, it's such a gift.

'So,' she said. 'These voices you hear. These people you see. Tell me about them.'

And I did, as I've told you, bit by bit. She walked the round mile with me and heard and saw her own version of things. And, of course, there were fragments to gather up afterwards, as with everything. The way you put carrots and turnips and onions and meat into a pot and then call it a stew. Grandfather, and my very early infant memory of him on a Clydesdale horse. That summer's day out at the peats with Mary Ann playing hide and seek behind the stack. Mum telling the story of Catrìona and Eòghainn again on the night she died. All those voices I heard downstairs when I was a child in bed, telling of fairies and bogles and ghosts and demons and knights and witches and kings. How the poor boy from Vatersay married the King of Greece's daughter and how the poor girl from Mingulay married the King of Ireland's son, who could slay seven warriors with one cut of his sword this way, and seventy-seven of them with the cut of his sword that way. Even Alladin and his magic lamp. None of them ever age. They keep me young, for when I speak to them I'm always the age I was when I first heard and saw them, and they haven't aged a day.

I got corresponding more often with Mr Haas. At first bits and pieces and odds and ends about the drawing room window which needed re-glazed, and the slates on the gable end which needed replaced and the garden grounds which needed weeded and harrowed and ploughed and re-seeded and he told me to go ahead and do these things. Which I did.

Then he sent me this letter:

Dear Mr MacDonald

Your story of The *Fuamhaire* and the Castle tells me that I am the *Fuamhaire*. Of course I can argue that I have earned my money – who hasn't? That's not the point. The point is: I heard that story from you some years ago and have never forgotten it. You probably don't know that I listened through the open window of the big house as you told the story on a fine spring morning to your cows. It was such a beautiful, still day. As far as I know, no one else was listening. But from that moment I've never locked the house. Feel free to use it as you wish. My only request is that you leave it vacant every Fall (your September) in case I or any of my friends

would like to visit. I only ever feel at home there when I'm away from it. A nostalgia for something I never knew was lost. Unlike Mrs Chisholm. I hope you will understand.
Sincerely,
Wendell Haas.

So there you have it, the offer to live in the sad *Fuamhaire's* castle.

13

THE LAST STATION before we get back home is *Tobar nam Ban* (The Well of the Women), where the old village well was before water got piped into everyone's homes. It's now only used by me and Maisie and the herd for one last drink before we set off towards the byre. I've fixed a rubber pipe from the well to fill their trough. I use the scallop shell that a pedlar woman, *Brighde nam Beann* (Bridget of the Bens), left for wandering pilgrims years and years ago.

The well is thirty feet deep – I've measured it with a rod – and still produces the finest water in the area, but folk can't be bothered walking out to it, and why would they when good clean water runs in gallons from the taps in their houses?

Though it's not the same. This water is clear and sparkling compared to the insipid water I have at home, which Nurse MacLeish says to me is safer and cleaner for me. As if anything could be cleaner than something coming straight from the earth. It also gives me the weather forecast. When the water rises in the well dry weather is coming. When it shrinks, it's going to rain.

The water from the well is also holy. Saint Fillan personally blessed it when he visited here in the 8th century to establish the Christian faith. The remains of his *Cill* (Cell/Church) are high up on the hill, from where you can see forever. He carved an inscription on the church's lintel: *Mo Dhia agus m' Èirinn bheannaichte* (My beloved God and Ireland).

'Those were the days,' Grandfather said, 'when we worked the land and wise men prayed for us.'

I like going to church. It comforts me. I have a bath every Saturday night. It's nice to put on my Sunday suit. It's all I do. I don't have to do anything else, because Jesus has done it all for me. The communion wafer assures me of that. I used to wonder at the older women who couldn't get through the Hail Mary without drawing breath. But now I'm that age myself, I don't wonder any more. I can get down to 'blessed is the fruit of thy womb, Jesus', where it's right and proper to breathe and pause and then continue together, Holy Mary mother of God pray for us sinners now and at the hour of our death Amen. Then I look up again. Hector MacLeod still wears a kipper tie with a picture of a kipper on it. He always sits in the third pew near the front to the right.

Tobar nam Ban is a healing well. I know that because any time I've been unwell, I've come here and knelt and prayed and taken of the water and risen healed. Everyone used to believe that, and some used to do it, but no one now does. I don't know why. I presume because Nurse MacLeish and Doctor MacLaren are the new wise men and help them instead. But Saint Fillan was loved by the people because he was particularly good at healing, and my grandfather told me why.

'When Fillan was a young lad just like you,' he said, 'he went on a journey to France.'

'Where's that?' I asked.

'Over the water,' Grandfather said. 'And the reason he went to France was to see this famous doctor who was said to be able to heal all kinds of diseases.'

'Even if you were dying?' I asked.

'Even if you were dying,' Grandfather said. 'Even if you were dead.'

'Wow!'

'So when Fillan arrived in France and saw this doctor, you know what the doctor said to him?'

I shook my head.

'"If you're from Boisdale, would you go back there and get a snake which is lying under the big stone next to the well and carry her back to France to me?"'

'Now, Donald,' said Grandfather. 'This snake was the king of snakes. There was a difference between him and all other snakes, because he was completely white from the tip of the head to the tip of the tail. Fillan promised that he would try to do that and returned to Boisdale to the exact place asked of him, and he found the snake under a stone as the man said.

'He caught him and put him in a kettle and carried him away. Now, when the other snakes saw that he'd taken their king, they slithered after him. But Fillan knew that if he put seven streams between himself and the other snakes, he would be safe. He managed that, and escaped, and made his way back to France and reached the healer's house with the kettle and the snake.

'The other man was very happy to see him, and as soon as he saw Fillan he put the snake into a three-legged pot filled with water on a big fire which he brought to a boil. Now, Donald, here's the thing – he had to go out for something, so he told Fillan to stir the pot with a stick until he returned. But he warned him not to drink a single drop of the brew!

'Yet Fillan was so tired from the long journey that he fell asleep. The pot boiled over and the brew spilled onto the floor and his hand and fingers, and he was in such pain from the scalding brew that he stuck his fingers in his mouth and inadvertently sucked up the liquid coating his hand. And it was from that drop that he got the power and strength for teaching and healing – the thing that the French healer wanted to preserve for himself!

'When he came here he blessed this well, and in those days it was called *Tobar Fhialain* (Fillan's Well), though it's not called that nowadays, but *Tobar nam Ban*.'

'Why?' I asked him.

'Because,' he said, 'over time, only women went to the well. The men were busy fishing and away at sea and only women gathered there with their pails and buckets to carry the water home. They sipped of the waters when they were there, and as a result lived to a great age.'

Sometimes the blessing comes by accident. By providence. When I was at sea, one of the cooks was a young man from Canada called Aaron. He was the only one who helped when I got into scrapes. When I finally signed off from the Merchant Navy in Liverpool to go home to Mum for the last time, he came up to me and gave me this blue ribband and said, 'Donald, always wear this and remember me.'

And I do. I pin it onto every shirt I wear, so that he's with me every day as I watch over the herd. Strange how I can always see Catriona and Mary Ann's face but I can't remember what Aaron looked like. Maybe, like Saint Fillan who left us the well, the tassel is enough. It tells me of his goodness and kindness.

On quiet evenings I light a fire outside and watch if any snakes appear. They never do. I burn paper and rubbish in the fire, not because I have to get rid of it, but because I like to see and smell the smoke as it rises in the garden. The smell of woodsmoke is best and, depending on the wind, the smoke goes in spirals or clouds. It's best when it rises straight up into the air, for that's a sign of good clear days to come. I know it gives pleasure to neighbours who see it rise into the air, reminding them of their childhood when they too, with friends, lit fires and jumped through the flames on St John's Eve as a blessing.

14

MAISIE AND THE herd are always happy to see the byre at the end of the day. It's a familiar, safe place to them. I always make sure it's nice and clean, with fresh straw and some ventilation and tubs of water (drawn from the well) at both ends. I grow turnips for them and they could live on them in the same way I could live happily on potatoes. I give them some oats and crushed turnips and vitamin pellets before milking them, which is the best part of the day. We're all tired, but happy. We've gone all the way round the world in a day and returned home safely.

I milk by hand. You squeeze the teat to the beat of your heart to get the rhythm right. Maisie first, so that the others know how to behave when their turn comes. Standing steady with a calmness that all is well and that they're giving of their best. I sing to them because that makes the milk richer and creamier. Lullabies mostly, for these quieten us all, bring us back to our mother's breast. Small soft sounds cradle us towards kindness. The herd smell me and I smell mint.

'*Bà bà mo leanabh beag*

Bà bà mo leanabh beag
Gur dè a ghaoil a nì mi dhut
Is eagal orm nach fhàs thu.
Gur dè a ghaoil a nì mi dhut
Gur dè a ghaoil a nì mi dhut
Gur dè a ghaoil a nì mi dhut
Is eagal orm nach fhàs thu.
Bà bà mo leanabh beag
Bà bà mo leanabh beag
Gur dè a ghaoil a nì mi dhut
Is eagal orm nach fhàs thu.'

They like that one. Especially the young ones. I watch them rocking backwards like a child about to fall asleep as I sing the lullaby again and again. But sometimes I sing ones for myself, which Maisie and the older ones like too, as if we're at a cèilidh together, singing to one another. I sing it for Mary Ann.

'*Fhir a' chinn dhuibh, hó hó...*
Man with the curly black hair,
And the curly locks,
And the white neck,
Little do I know
What has kept you from me:
My lack of cattle,
My small herd,
There is no black cow,
No red cow either,
Nor any cow in my fold.'

When Maisie and the herd are milked, they rest. I go into the house and drink a jug of the milk fresh from the udder and then have my meal of mutton, cabbage or turnip and potatoes and sit by the fire for a while. And gravy. There must be gravy. Bisto is okay, but I make the best myself from the beef or mutton fat juice with butter, salt and pepper. On Sundays, instead of beef and mutton, I eat salted herring. Sometimes I make pancakes for myself, toasting them on top of the stove. My mother used to say you'd know what kind of person you were dealing with from their choice of potatoes.

I had a choice to make. To stay as I'd been for the past fifty years or to become the new Lord of the Manor. To accept or reject Wendell Haas's offer. It was providential. Like St Fillan's great gift. The gift of chance. And was it really that much of a change anyway? Aren't we always ourselves, whether in a cave or in a castle, in rags or riches? Maisie and the herd would be Maisie and the herd whether grazing in England's green and pleasant land, as I've heard sung, as much as here in this bare and barren one.

And so, sitting there by the peat fire that night, I decided. I wasn't going to be like Eòghainn and run away and regret it all my days. Or the way I turned away from Mary Ann and all was lost. Lost so much that we couldn't even trust our own dreams any more. I believe now that Mary Ann was part of the fairy knoll filled with eternal youth and happiness. Maybe others can't change, but at least I had a chance. You have to give everything a chance to be.

I would become Caretaker of the Big House. Isn't that what I've been all along? The caretaker of Maisie and the herd. Of Rover and Wilhelmina, despite her proud air of independence. Of the family house and croft, and all those memories of horses and carts and the way grandfather used to sharpen the scythe with the whetting stone and anvil and hammer. A caretaker of everything I'd seen and heard and learned in heaven and on earth.

But this caretaking was of a different order. Taking care of someone else's goods and chattels and whatever memories and hopes and dreams were in them. It would be like working for a bank or as a clerk for an insurance company. A flunkey, running after the master's horse and doing his bidding. *Gille-tòine*, we call him in Gaelic – an arse-boy, ever at the beck and call of the owner. But this would be different. There was no master, or at least he was two thousand miles away across the wide Atlantic. And I'm no flunkey.

I refused to go and stay in the Big House. I couldn't. Instead, I agreed to go across every day and take care of things. I sold four of the herd, but kept Maisie and the youngest calf and bullock, for old times' sake. They stayed in the old barn and walked across to the Big House every day to graze on the beautifully manicured orchard lawn which I re-seeded with clover especially for them. They were in heaven. Maybe they believed I could always do more than what seems possible. I hope so.

When I say 'orchard', it doesn't exist anymore, except

as a word. It was established by Sir Archibald Sinclair when he first bought the house and brought with him a fellow called Grimstone as gardener. Grimstone and the local tenant labourers, each paid with a boll of meal, built the walled garden and planted the apple trees. But when Sir Archibald and Grimstone died the work stopped and the orchard was invaded by sheep who grazed everything to the ground so that all that remains is the name. You can only get apples now out in the shop, but they're tasteless, so I just make use of what's around, gathering the blaeberries that grow on the bushes out in the midst of the stream when I want to eat fruit or sweeten the Sunday pudding.

I loved looking after the house and its grounds in those early days. It had been left to decay for too long, and I took great pride in restoring it to its former glory. Some of it was simple – a matter of cleaning up and polishing all the beautiful old furniture and gilded mirrors. I liked how I looked in the huge one in the drawing room which covered the whole wall from side to side to side and from floor to ceiling. It was like seeing myself beyond space and time, because when I stood there and looked at my image it was only part of a wonderful whole: the majestic stags' horns hanging on the wall above me and the magnificent tapestries that gave the impression I was standing in some vine-filled valley in Italy or somewhere like that rather than in this bare rocky island of ours where nothing grows well except potatoes.

Mr Haas had sent another letter saying that friends

of his were on a cruise ship and would be calling in a month's time. As a special favour, would I out on the Highland outfit that was in the dressing room, so that they could see what a real old Highland Chieftain might have looked like. So I tried it on and thought I looked rather splendid in it. The MacDonald tartan kilt, the long sporran made of horse's hair, the shining silver *sgian dubh* in the stocking, the ruffed shirt and smart tweed jacket and, of course, the clan bonnet with the three eagle feathers. I know that the three feathers had been traditionally reserved for the chief, but these days of bowing to the chief were gone, and surely if anyone deserved to wear them, I did. A MacDonald since the time of Adam, who was the first of the clan.

But mostly I wore my old dungarees, for I spent most of the day working around the house and garden. The greenhouses were all overgrown, so it took me ages to get them into the best condition, but once I divided them into a nursery and a growth and a planting-out and blossoming area they worked wonderfully. Red and white and yellow roses here, nasturtiums and begonias there and – my favourites! – lilies everywhere. Their fragrance filled the air.

Inside, I renewed the v-lining on the library walls and replaced all the old wood on the window sashes so they could open and close as smoothly as the billiard balls moved on the table's newly restored green baize. I dusted off the portraits of the clan chiefs in their colourful kilts and feathers inside their gold frames on the walls. They looked down on me as if promising to look after me, like I did with Maisie and the herd. In the twilight, when the low sun came in through the west window, they softened like sheep safe in their fank for the night.

I only dressed up at weekends when all the tourists come in their busloads. Most of them off the cruise ships. Once they'd been driven around and seen the mountains and the long white stretches of sand and the old churches and had their lunch in the hotel, they stopped by to see the Big House. It's what they expect, and they delight in the colours I wear and take loads of pictures standing beside me to share with the world. I think it makes the world a happier place. They've come such a long way to see us, and many of the cruise passengers are the descendants of those who were so brutally cleared from here on the emigrant ships. I have decided they deserve this small reward, like having their photo taken with Maisie and her curved smooth Highland horns.

I sort of became the Laird of the Manor by default. Someone asked me one day what my title was and I said 'Lord Donald of Boisdale', and it stuck. I sent a form and a small cheque off to one of those addresses that grants you an ancestral title, and I got a badge and a gold-framed certificate back through the post declaring that I am officially '*Morair Bhaghasdail*' (Lord Boisdale) and that I'm also now the owner of a square foot of land in the great and tragic MacDonald territory of Glencoe. I'm not fooled by the certificate. We all know it's a bit of a game. No one owns anything, for the earth belongs unto the Lord, and all that it contains.

But when the tourists had gone, and I sat all alone in my kilt and feathers for a while in the great drawing room of the Big House, I cried. Maisie and the herd and Rover and Wilhelmina knew it when I got back home. They cosied themselves against me.

It's a good thing, said Nurse MacLeish, for it's years and years since I've cried, guarding everything like that giant in the castle behind a high wall. And now I've walked through the front door, and here it is in all its emptiness.

I felt like a layabout, though I kept myself busy polishing mirrors and dusting pictures and hoovering and repairing bits of broken door handles and making sure all the books in the library were in proper alphabetical order. I did them first by the title, from Aesop's Fables down to a book called *Zen and the Art of Motorcycle Maintenance*, but then changed the system so that the authors' name went first, from Aesop to Zhu Xi. It passed the time.

There were also so many clocks in the place, all of them silent and unmoving. Grandfather clocks and small square ones on shelves and big wall-mounted ones and an array of cuckoo clocks. I wound them all up and put them to the correct time, but within moments they were all telling me something different, some fast, some slow, some unmoving. I sat there listening to the dozens of tick-tocks as if time itself was in the room. I could hear my own heartbeat between the wooden cuckoos popping in and out. The only place where time stops is out there on the moor with Maisie and Rover and the herd, not in here in this ticking cage.

What an *Amadan*. A *Gloic*. But not in that foolish and idiotic way, for maybe a fool and an idiot don't realise the darkness of their ways? But in the real sense of shaming myself. Becoming less than I ought to be. Like the man who sold his inheritance for a pot of stew. I thought of a compromise, but knew it was doomed. I could keep caring for the Big House, but instead of showing visitors the tapestries and the Persian carpets and the library and the snooker room I could take them on my round mile and show them *Cnoc nan Òran* and *Tobar nam Ban* and *Lòn a' Phùinnsein* and the ruins of Catrìona's cottage. Names that only I know now. To the younger generation it's just the moor. Where the wind pylons are and where the spaceport will go. Though I have heard some of the children call it 'Donald's Mile'. Which is an honour, I think, because they don't laugh when they say it.

Nurse MacLeish brought me to my senses.

'They're all laughing at you,' she said to me one day.

'They've always laughed at me,' I said.

'But that was because you were real. Yourself. Now they laugh at you because you're not.'

The next weekend I stood and looked at myself properly in the full-length mirror in the hallway and felt embarrassed. Dressed up like a doll in this ridiculous outfit invented by King George and his friends, unlike my ancestors who had marched off to their clan wars and in the footsteps of the bonny Prince in the rags they were wearing – the plaid over their shoulders and their daggers by their sides – to defend his name and their honour. It would be better to disrobe and walk naked through the village than shame myself any longer, so – like David before Goliath – I took off the coat of armour and returned to my sling: my overalls and bunnet and stick, and I swear to you that Maisie and the remnants of the herd came running to me as if I was a man returned, made young and well and healthy again, from the fairy knoll itself.

15

SO I CAME back to where I started. I'm not a reader of books that aren't atlases or don't have pictures in them, but the one book I took with me – stole – from the library in the Big House was *The Great Gatsby*. I like the drawing on the cover. A big house and a long green lawn just like Mr Haas's property, and then this figure, all dressed up and looking ever so elegant, at the bottom of the steps, looking lost. As if he's got no friends in the world. In his golden cage. He doesn't quite fit into his surroundings. Doesn't belong there. A country man in town, without cows. Like a man from South Uist finding himself in the North. Mr Haas. And me.

The truth is that you can't have it both ways. You can't have your cake and eat it, as they say. The price was too high. Circumstances change you. Despite all my excuses and justifications, I couldn't be the same man in a kilt as in my oilskins, in the castle as in the byre. A cowherd pretending to be a laird. I don't believe in God because I've seen miracles or because it comforts me but because he's as real to me as the wellington boots I stand in. He's everywhere, from the gurgling sound my tea makes as I pour into my cup first thing every morning to the wild way the wind sweeps against the gable end of the house every night. The miracle is that I can lie down to sleep at night and get up every morning believing it's worth getting up again. To stir the fire and boil the kettle and have my porridge and feed Wilhemina and Rover and to greet Maisie and the herd, again and again, for our new day's adventure.

The problem I have with Mr Haas is that he is so absent. Thousands of miles away across the ocean in his own wee world. Not like Maisie and the herd and Rover and Wilhelmina and Janet Smith, forever singing and chattering just over the brae, part of the daily music of my life. I don't hear Mr Haas whistling in the morning or see him waving goodnight from the end of the byre in the twilight as Old Smith used to do before he went away. There is only his big empty house, which is no church where we can all sing and worship together. Blessed are the poor in spirit for heaven is theirs. Miss Smith will be there with her hens in her own special mansion. I'm pretty sure she won't want a mansion, but a wee cottage with a nice green sward for her sheep and a free-running area with a puddly pond for her ducks and hens.

I missed Maisie and the whole herd, and Rover was as miserable as hell, sitting whining at the door as if all the other animals in the world had deserted him and gone elsewhere and he was left alone with nothing to do except lie there on the big slate step. And that's no life for a collie dog. Wilhelmina curled her tail with that look that said, 'You come and go, Donald. For God's sake, make your mind up and stay over at that big house or be like me, content to sit here purring in my own domain.' She lives quite happily under the chair and on the windowsill. When I'm not there, on the chair itself.

Because I was spending a bit more time fixing things around the big house we all saw a bit less of each other. I'm not sure about Wilhelmina, but the rest of us all missed one another.

The cows, especially, missed the mile. The full, round mile genetically ran through them, as it did through me, and I could see in their eyes that look beyond the sweet orchard towards the wild, bare moor where their mother and their mother's mother and on and on had walked and grazed and paused and pissed and drunk water and ate seaweed down by the shore and the sweet grass by the loch and the rough grass by the rock where *Mac Talla nan Creag* always spoke when spoken to.

What happened was that our routine, which is to say our world, was broken. It reminded me of Old Smith, the joiner, who was forced by the Council in his old age to move from his decaying thatched house to his daughter's new home at the other end of the village. He died shortly after. Of a broken heart. He complained that it was like being transported to the other side of the world. To move an inch is to emigrate a mile, as Campbell the village *bàrd* once put it.

Animals sense things. Maisie and the herd continued to graze happily as I left them for times to do something or other at the big house, but they knew things were different. Maybe they trusted me a bit less. The land itself remembered our absences. Since we visited them less frequently, *Tobar nam Ban* and *Lòn a' Phuinnsein* and *Cnoc nan Òran* all seemed quieter on our return. Not because they were in the huff, but because they were becoming used to different circumstances. The grass grew slightly longer, the water higher and the fairy hollow quieter, as if the little people themselves had stopped singing and playing because they didn't believe in my coming to listen to them anymore.

I tried to replace the round mile walk with the orchard walk, but it was never the same. Too tame, and though I tried to make friends with the little fish in the garden pond and with the trees and the swaying leaves. I missed the bareness of the cattle walk, as if I was replacing the salvation of the Stations of the Cross with the ease and comfort of an armchair.

I saw others in the big, gilded mirrors, but they were strangers and looked away when I approached, or spoke in ways I didn't understand, and when I spoke to them they looked through me, or over my shoulders, towards some distant land of their own. They had their own story to tell, and I was unable to walk into the mirror to hear it. Maybe if I had persevered, but I didn't have the strength anymore.

One night, as the full moon shone over Easabhal, I left the Big House and walked across the land through the open fields and over the stone walls and the little stream and the river to the old house which lay glowing, like a sea urchin shell, in the reddish light of the moon. And as I approached, I could hear the faint sound of singing and taste the fragrance of mint, and when I arrived the fire was lit, and her voice calling to me, '*Thig a-staigh a Dhòmhnaill.*' ('Come in, Donald.') '*Bidh acras a' mhonaidh ort.*' ('You'll have the hunger of the moor.') '*Trobhad, suidh sìos, agus gabh rudeigin.*' ('Come, sit down, and eat something.')

'Then we'll talk all about it, won't we, my love?'

16

IT ALL HAPPENED because of the garden. I never had time for it. Well, never really bothered with it. Earth should be used for growing hay and corn and wheat, or potatoes and carrots and cabbages, not grass and flowers and trees. These grow naturally in the fields and on the moor and machair. The earth feeds us as long as we feed it. I carry up bales of seaweed and spread it where I plant things, and dig drains and ditches to make sure it gets enough water, but not too much. It's just like looking after Maisie and the herd.

Mum kept the garden, but it was so difficult to grow anything nice in it. She would plant seeds and the first wind would blow them away. Occasionally she would get rose saplings through the post, but no sooner were they planted than they were trampled by the sheep or eaten by deer or rabbits.

'We need to fix these walls,' she'd say, and we'd make an effort to lift up the stones again which had fallen down in the last storm and had been trampled by the cows. It was an endless task, when so much else had to be done to survive.

'Flour is what you need, not flowers,' Grandfather

said, and that hovered over us like a necessity.

So when Mum died I didn't even make the gesture of looking after the garden. It became overgrown, and when things broke down or I needed a new axle for the cart or tractor, the old one was inevitably dumped in the front garden to gather weeds and rust. Nurse MacLeish started coming over on Saturdays because she wanted to deal with it.

'That could be such a pretty garden, Donald,' she said. 'It's in such a beautiful spot and if it was tidied up it would look lovely. Do you mind...?' she asked.

Of course I minded, but I didn't want to hurt her.

'Whatever,' I said. 'But why?'

She looked at me, and for the first time I didn't see Nurse MacLeish, but Patricia Campbell.

'Because,' she said, 'of your mother. She was such a good friend of my mother's. She used to call in at our house on Saturdays on the way back from the shop. She always brought in a handful of wildflowers she'd picked from the roadside on the way. Daffodils or orchids or daisies or whatever was growing wild at the time. I loved the colours she brought with her, yellow and green and blue and purple and all kinds, and we'd sit together at the scullery window arranging them into little bunches to put in a vase. That's why.' It's so difficult to get to know another human being. It's like learning a new geography, a whole new world past Maisie and the herd, beyond memory and myself.

We worked on the garden together, of course. The first thing was to get rid of all the rubbish that had gathered and lain there over the years and to fix the drystone wall, which had caved-in here and there and completely fallen in places. Bits of engines, empty tins of oil, rotting battens of wood, tractor tyres, odds-and-ends of cardboard, a few broken creels and all the weeds that I'd allowed to flourish over the years.

It took me forever to move things compared to Patricia. Not because I'm lazy, but if a thing (say the shaft of an old scythe) had lain there for scores of years, it earned a permanence. If I left it there it would be there forever, which meant that nothing had ever changed and that things were and would always be as they had always been, with Mum singing away in the kitchen and Grandfather coming home shortly with the horses from the machair.

'To leave something to be itself is the best we can do,' I said to her.

Patricia would have none of it.

'The only thing that matters is what we do now,' she'd say, and start moving things until I was shamed to moving them with her.

What a bonfire we had that first Saturday evening, as Patricia cooked some sausages for us on the small camping stove she brought over. The combined smell of burning rubber and sizzling sausages has been the scent of life ever since.

The next few Saturdays we dug up the garden. I with the spade and Patricia coming after with the hoe and rake and barrow. We carted all the stuff down to the back of the byre for the compost heap. It's best when the steam rises from it and you can watch the worms and beetles and ants and flies and snails and slugs work their ways through it, leaving it all juicy for feeding the vegetable patch later on. It's odd. When I carried a barrowful across to the heap the load seemed heavy. But when she carried the same amount the barrow moved lightly, as if she was carrying feathers. 'It's yoga flow,' she said. Whatever that meant. 'Just means the barrow does all the work,' she said, tipping the contents into the compost. Then there was the drystone wall to fix and renew, which took the best part of that long summer, as I lifted up the fallen stones and gathered new ones from down the shore and from old ruined byres and gave them to Patricia, who was in charge of the wall itself.

'It's just like nursing,' she said. 'You clean the wound here, and then cover it with elastoplast and it heals itself.'

It was wonderful to watch an old, disused thing being made new. Where needed, we stripped the whole wall back to the bare earth and re-laid the corner and bottom stones good and proper so that they sat solid and secure. Then the ones on top fitted into the crevices so that nothing moved, or was shoogly. She trusted the stones.

'Och, it's just gravity,' she said.

And – perhaps above all, I don't know, but I think so – laying them so that they would look beautiful. By which I mean steady and balanced, so that each stone complemented the one next to it and above it and below it. So that, from a distance, the drystone wall looks like it is made of one – or a thousand – stones matching each other the way in which a cow – or a thousand head of grazing cattle – look as if they were placed there by God himself from the beginning of time for our joy and salvation. There is nothing on earth like a well-built drystone wall.

'As long as it's true to itself, it will not fall down,' she said when it was finished.

Once the wall was up we took to planting the garden. Patricia conceded me a corner for onions and shallots, but argued that the main part should simply be used for the glory of God.

'Roses here, and lilies there, and nasturtiums over in that sheltered corner, and – of course – a rowan tree here by the door, and let's plant some birch and hazel and alder over in that corner where the prevailing wind is.'

She reminded me of the need to plant and sow according to the waning or waxing moon. To plant the vegetables that grow underground – things like potatoes and onions and turnips – in the dark of the moon so that they root down well, and the things that grow above ground, like lettuce and peas and stuff like that, in the light of the moon so that they grow upwards as the moon increases.

They've all grown now. Not because some miracle has taken place ('though of course it has,' she keeps saying), but because we've nurtured and sheltered and pruned and looked after them all, protecting them as best we can from rabbits (we're endlessly filling in holes in the ground and gaps in the wall) and deer and sheep, and even from my herd. It's nice to see things which I don't plan to eat grow just as well as the potatoes do.

I catch Maisie sometimes standing on the other side of the garden wall looking enviously into the garden, and all that pretty green grass which would be so luscious to chew on, and all those pretty flowers and vegetables which would be such a marvellous feast for herself and her children. At those times I stroke her back and sing to her and she seems happy that I'm happy. It's strange. When I'm with Maisie and the herd there is nothing else but Maisie and the herd, and when I'm now with Patricia there is nothing else but her. Not even Nurse MacLeish.

She's a woman of smells too. Takes cuttings from the garden and from the machair and moor and roadside ditches when she's out and about and puts them in empty jam jars on shelves and sills and in nooks and crannies throughout the house so that we remember there's an outside when we're inside. She also bought me a bottle of aftershave from the Frenchwoman who lives at the other end of the island and makes candles and perfumes. The one Patricia got me is called *Faiche* (Meadow), which says that after I use it I will smell like an Autumn day after the hay has been newly cut, though it smells to me more like that air spray they use on the ferry to try and sweeten things up when they wipe the tables after a storm. So I've just started growing my beard long again.

We take it in turns to herd now. I went to see MacPherson the auctioneer to get back up to the magic number. I take Maisie and the seven cows on our mile-long walk on Mondays and Wednesdays and Fridays and Patricia takes them on Tuesdays and Thursdays and then we both take them on Saturdays. Sundays, of course, are still our days of rest, though we permit ourselves to prune the roses when in season, and pick whatever flowers are growing and take them in to put in the glass vase in the kitchen. In the evenings, when the western sun filters in through the kitchen window, the picked flowers display all their light, shimmering yellow and gold and red and indigo onto the wall above the stove.

Patricia comes in.

'How's Donald?' she says.

I smile at her.

'Donald and his seven cows, I mean,' she says, putting the kettle on.

Acknowledgements

MY THANKS TO Kapka Kassabova who encouraged me to write Donald's story and for her generous words on reading it. To Angus and Judy Martin of Kintyre who read earlier versions of the work, proofread it, and suggested important textual changes. I'm especially grateful to Angus for prompting me to write the concluding chapter, and for his informative introduction, setting the story into its cultural context. My thanks to Gwyneth Findlay who edited the book with patience and insight. To Gavin MacDougall and the Luath team – Jennie Renton, Amy Turnbull, Kira Dowie and Scott Kemp for all their work. *Tapadh leibh uile.*

Luath Press Limited

committed to publishing well written books worth reading

LUATH PRESS takes its name from Robert Burns, whose little collie Luath (*Gael.*, swift or nimble) tripped up Jean Armour at a wedding and gave him the chance to speak to the woman who was to be his wife and the abiding love of his life. Burns called one of the 'Twa Dogs' Luath after Cuchullin's hunting dog in Ossian's *Fingal*. Luath Press was established in 1981 in the heart of Burns country, and is now based a few steps up the road from Burns' first lodgings on Edinburgh's Royal Mile. Luath offers you distinctive writing with a hint of unexpected pleasures.

Most bookshops in the UK, the US, Canada, Australia, New Zealand and parts of Europe, either carry our books in stock or can order them for you. To order direct from us, please send a £sterling cheque, postal order, international money order or your credit card details (number, address of cardholder and expiry date) to us at the address below. Please add post and packing as follows: UK – £1.00 per delivery address; overseas surface mail – £2.50 per delivery address; overseas airmail – £3.50 for the first book to each delivery address, plus £1.00 for each additional book by airmail to the same address. If your order is a gift, we will happily enclose your card or message at no extra charge.

Luath Press Limited
543/2 Castlehill
The Royal Mile
Edinburgh EH1 2ND
Scotland
Telephone: 0131 225 4326 (24 hours)
Email: sales@luath.co.uk
Website: www.luath.co.uk